NO ANGELS

Robert Swindells left school at the age of fifteen and joined the Royal Air Force at seventeen-and-a-half. After his discharge, he worked at a variety of jobs before training and working as a teacher. He is now a full-time writer and lives with his wife, Brenda, on the Yorkshire moors. Robert Swindells has written many books for young people, and in 1984 was the winner of the Children's Book Award and the Other Award for his novel *Brother in the Land*. He won the Children's Book Award for a second time in 1990 with *Room 13*, and in 1994 *Stone Cold* won the Carnegie Medal and the Sheffield Book Award.

ROBERT SWINDELLS
NO ANGELS

PUFFIN BOOKS

PUFFIN BOOKS

Published by the Penguin Group
Penguin Books Ltd, 80 Strand, London WC2R 0RL, England
Penguin Putnam Inc., 375 Hudson Street, New York, New York 10014, USA
Penguin Books Australia Ltd, 250 Camberwell Road, Camberwell, Victoria 3124, Australia
Penguin Books Canada Ltd, 10 Alcorn Avenue, Toronto, Ontario, Canada M4V 3B2
Penguin Books India (P) Ltd, 11 Community Centre, Panchsheel Park, New Delhi – 110 017, India
Penguin Books (NZ) Ltd, Cnr Rosedale and Airborne Roads, Albany, Auckland, New Zealand
Penguin Books (South Africa) (Pty) Ltd, 24 Sturdee Avenue, Rosebank 2196, South Africa

Penguin Books Ltd, Registered Offices: 80 Strand, London WC2R 0RL, England

www.penguin.com

First published 2003
4

Set in Monotype Baskerville and Arial
Typeset by Rowland Phototypesetting Ltd, Bury St Edmunds, Suffolk

Made and printed in England by Clays Ltd, St Ives plc

British Library Cataloguing in Publication Data
A CIP catalogue record for this book is available from the British Library

ISBN 0-141-31462-1

Nikki

The day I decide to split, Kirsty sends this: WASSU? ItsYaLif but RUsureNowIsTRItTIm? CUatSCL?

I don't know about *right* time. When your mum's boyfriend's trying to get in your pants and your mum won't believe you it's *time*, that's all. And no, Kirsty, you *won*'t see me at school. I answer: GOdblBadTIms MOvnOn ll KIT.

Moving on. Sounds easy, right? Romantic even. I feel pretty cool too, standing on the corner with my bag between my feet, phone in hand, texting. I picture myself tonight, in a room of my own with a lock on the door somewhere north of the river where Ronnie can't find me. That's his name by the way: Ronnie. Call me Dad he says, like I would. Anyway, he's history as far as I'm concerned; a fragment of the past as somebody once said.

I haven't thought it through. You don't at fourteen with a thirty-something perv breathing down your neck.

Nick

It com so cold middle of December Jack sez, wiv fings so tite I gotta let you go, Nick. Jack's a coster. I bin his boy from twelve and I'm two year older now. He bin treat me rite, him and Bet. She's Jack's wife.

I sez, tite? Wot about Ma, Connie and little Fan? Tite wiv you's titer wiv us.

I know, he sez, and I'm sorry. Here. He presses a gen in my hand. That's a shilling in coster langwige. That'll get yer a few dinners, he sez. Bestist I can do. I looks in his eyes and knows it's the troof. Fings'll buck up boy, he sez, com spring.

How to *liv* till spring, that's the trick. How to fill Ma's belly, and the little gels. In good times Ma gets needlework and Connie helps wiv it, but ther's none to be had since the cold set in. Cold? You never seen such cold. The river, wot never had so much as a *dab* of ice on it befor in Ma's lifetime, is solid from bank to bank, so that a cove mite walk from Sent Pauls to the new cut wivout settin foot on a bridge. Last nite some chap in the beer-shop – a scholard – reads owt a bit in the paper sez the winter of fifty-free – that's *this* winter – will go down in histry. Aye, yells won wag, and we'll all go down *wiv* it if it don't let up direcly.

He was rite, that wag. Plenty gon down alreddy: down

the workhouse, down the churchyard, down to ell for ought I know. Ther's undreds wivowt work, wivowt dosh, wivowt a roof.

Now *we*'re of that happy band, Ma, the gels and me.

Nikki

A room of my own with a lock on the door. Yeah right. Here's what actually happens. I ride the tube to King's X and tramp the streets, looking for windows with cards in them. ROOM TO LET. When you're not looking they seem to be everywhere. I find a few, but when I knock either nobody's home or they take one look at me and say it's taken. Let it dear, five minutes ago. Shame.

It's my age, see? They look at me and their brain goes, *runaway*. Nobody's going to let to someone dodgy: they don't need to. I start at half-nine and by eleven I'm knackered. Not giving up though. Well I *can*'t, can I? I find a coffee shop, break into my savings to take the weight off my feet for a bit.

Oh yes, I've got dosh. Seventy-seven pounds. Started saving as soon as I knew I was going to have to leave. Weeks ago that was, November fifth. Guy Fawkes' night. Mum'd taken our Marie to the fire up the Victoria, that's the local pub. They have a big do: firework display, baked potatoes, beer at happy-hour prices, chips for the kids. I'd gone every year since I was little but this time I didn't feel interested, and anyway the weather'd turned cold so I decided to stay in. Big mistake, but not my fault.

Ronnie never misses a chance to go up the pub. Never. So naturally I assumed he'd be going with Mum and Marie, but when I said I was staying in he suddenly remembered some soccer match on telly. There *was* a match: Chelsea v Arsenal.

4

He hadn't mentioned it earlier, that's all. I mean, Mum'd assumed he'd be going with her. She was disappointed. I don't get it, she said. Why didn't you say?

I understood all right, but I couldn't say anything. She's crazy about Ronnie: he can do no wrong. And I couldn't change my mind could I, it'd be too obvious. So off goes Mum with Marie, and I mumble something about homework and go up to my room. There's no lock on the door but it's *my* room, has been since I was twelve. Nobody comes in my room unless I invite them, not even Mum. I *have* got some homework as it happens, so I swap my school skirt for a pair of jeans, switch on my computer and settle down, shoving uneasiness to the back of my mind along with the flashes and bangs outside.

And he comes up. I've not been working five minutes when the catch clicks. I turn the swivel-chair and he's in the doorway and I say, what d'you want?

He laughs softly, closes the door behind him, leans on it. I think you know the answer to that one, he says. You're a big girl now, pretty one too. We could make this a really *special* bonfire night, you and me. One to remember. He comes towards me saying, *remember remember the fifth of November*. His voice sounds funny: hoarse. He stretches out a hand and starts stroking my hair. He's done it before; it gets him worked up. I don't want him touching me but I can't move. I'm paralysed. A part of my mind wonders if this is what it's like for girls who turn up strangled. I bet they're paralysed too, before they die.

His palm slides over my scalp. I have straight blonde hair, worn long. He lifts a handful, lets it slip through his fingers like he's feeling the quality. The expression on his face scares me enough so I duck away, hit his hand with my fist and get up off the chair. Ouch! He pretends to nurse his wrist, then laughs.

5

Nice one Nikki, he says, backing me into the corner by the window. I like a bit of spirit in a gel. Then he closes in and his hands are all over and I know why I changed into jeans.

I fight my way out of the corner but he grabs me and throws me down on the bed. I roll across it and make a dash for the door. I beat him by a fraction and hit the stairs running. He doesn't follow but stands looking over the bannister going, whatsamatter darling it's just a bit of fun, just a joke. Nikki? *Nikki*?

I run out of the house. It's freezing, I've nothing on over my school blouse and I head for the Victoria meaning to tell Mum, but when I get there I can't. I just can't. She says, you must be daft our Nikki, coming out like that in this weather. It's all right Mum, I say, I'm warm enough by the fire.

Actually I'm freezing, but I have to tough it out till Mum decides it's Marie's bedtime and we walk back together. When we get in, Ronnie's got the kettle on. Good time? he asks like nothing's happened, and Mum hugs him and says, lovely sweetheart, but lovelier coming home to you, and that's when I know it's time to go.

Nick

We always was 'spectable, us Webleys. Never bin on the parish, nor never *would* be neever. My father was Daniel Webley the carpenter. We'd our own house: the *hole* house, not won poky room like now, and we ate and drest as well as any workin fambly in Vesminster. I was in ragged school but *not* in rags, wery fair at readin and cipherin but can't wait to com fourteen, join father at the carpentin.

Then he falls off of a roof owt Marybon way and killt, and the fambly com down too, only slower. Connie six, Fan noffing but a babe. Ma takes in sewin work, I gets on nipperin reglar for Jack: good bunts but not enuff tween the two of us to keep from losin the house, tho Ma sewin till she can't see. We sells up, moves to this court callt Sharp's Rents which it's dark and smelly and full of thieves and beggars. Father'd weep, see wot his fambly com to.

Four in won room and lucky at that. Ovver rooms got seven eight peeple, ten even; some drunken, some idiot, won mad. Mad won's in the nex room, old cove call Jimmy o'Dowd, squats all day by the fire fryin a panful of saveloys tho ther's no saveloys, no pan and no fire. I can't get Jimmy o'Dowd owt of my hed, finks abowt him all the time. See, I knows wot'll com of him one day: get carted off to the madhouse wot toffs calls *asylum*, never com owt again. Always was scairt of that asylum, me. Sooner be drunken, cripple, anyfing. Sooner be *blind*.

So anyway we gets use to Sharp's Rents, its smells and low compny cos we *has* to. Ma workin hard, me and all, to find for rent and coals and grub, and little Connie's keepin the room clean, witch it's the only clean won in the house at that. Down but never owt, that's us.

Then com the cold.

Letter to the Sunday Telegraph

Sir

Your correspondent Mrs Marsden (24/11/02) asks why, in one of the most prosperous nations on earth, do we compel so many young people to live on the street. Allow me to counter the lady's question with one of my own, which I will then proceed to answer.

My question is, how do these young persons come to be on the street in the first place, and my answer is, by their own choice. There is no doubt in my mind that if a survey were carried out it would reveal that:

a. *The overwhelming majority of these so-called homeless youngsters are not homeless at all: they have perfectly good homes which they leave each morning in their scruffiest clothes in order to spend the day begging, which is a damn sight easier than working.*
b. *That the handful who are genuinely homeless have made themselves homeless, either because they refuse to accept the slightest degree of parental control, or because their parents have been rendered so feckless by the nanny state that there is no control, and none of the settled routines which make a house a home. In effect they were homeless already, though there was a roof of sorts over their heads.*

c. That the cash extorted from a gullible public by both these categories of young beggar is spent almost exclusively on drugs and alcohol, whose effects are guaranteed to render their consumers permanently unemployable.

d. That in every case, the homeless youngster might if he wished return to the parental home and resume a normal life, at the cost merely of conforming to the none too demanding norms of decent society.

What our young people need, Mrs Marsden, is fewer do-gooders, fewer corduroy-clad social workers, fewer so-called child psychologists smoking stubby pipes, fewer left-wing teachers and a great deal more good old-fashioned discipline.

Yours sincerely
Cleasby Nossiter

Nikki

I make my coffee last, remembering the fifth of November, gazing blankly out the window at people hurrying by. I need a plan. In fact the plan should've come first, but it's too late to say that now.

First priority has to be somewhere to stay. I'm beginning to realize knocking on doors is just a waste of time. I'm starting to think about Gran, and I know what *you*'re thinking. You're thinking oh, there's a *Gran*, so why all this tramping about, knocking on doors? Well, it isn't as easy as that because Gran's my *dad*'s mother, and my dad left us because he found out Mum was seeing Ronnie, which means Mum's a slag as far as Gran's concerned, and the daughter of a slag's gonna grow up to be another slag, isn't she? We've heard nothing from Gran Minton for two years, not even a Christmas card. And in case you're wondering about my *other* grandparents, Mum's mum and dad, well, they live in West Sussex and I can't go to them because *a*: it's the first place Mum'll check, *b*: they'd send me straight back, and *c*: they wouldn't believe my story about Ronnie because their daughter's far too smart to fall for a guy like that. Gran Minton on the other hand might believe because she *wants* to, because it'll seem like whatsit to her: poetic justice. Gran it is then, and hope she don't slam the door in my face.

Her place is in Camden: Arlington Road. It's not far and the weather's dry. I decide to walk. As I boogie on up Pancras Road

I tell myself it's just for a night or two. It might take Mum a while, but she's bound to call sooner or later and I can't ask Gran to lie for me. If I can just talk her into putting me up for a couple of nights so I can get my head together, I'll find a place of my own, plus some work that'll pay the rent.

Man, was I green.

She's out when I get there. I ring her bell a few times and some guy from upstairs comes down, half dressed. Mrs Minton's up the High Street, he says, shopping. He sounds pissed off, like I interrupted something. I start to say I'll wait in the hallway but he shuts the door, which he'd only opened a crack anyway. I hear him stamping back upstairs. I could go for a walk, try later, but my feet hurt so I sit down on the step. I look at my watch. Twenty to one. Lunchtime at school. I get my phone out, hoping Kirsty's is on.

Hi.

Nikki! Where the heck *are* you?

Oh, not far away. How you doing?

Never mind *me*. What's *goodbye to bad times* mean? How bad can it *be*?

Bad enough. Listen, I'll call you every day at half-twelve, right?

Okay but . . .

Make sure your phone's switched on. And if you see my mum, don't let on we're in touch, all right?

Yes okay but . . .

Catch you later, Kirsty. Bye.

I'm putting the phone in my bag when I spot Gran coming along the road with two bulging carriers. I can tell by the way she's walking they're heavy. I get up so she'll see me before she reaches the gateway. They don't like surprises, old ladies.

Hi, Gran.

Kirsty? She peers at me. I suppose I've changed in two years. What're you doing here? Shouldn't you be at school?

Yes Gran I should, only something's happened. Here, let me . . . I take the bags so she can find the key in her jacket pocket. She opens the door, steps inside, holds it for me.

Ta, Gran. I pull a face. These weigh a ton, what you been buying?

Just groceries. Tins're heavy. Put them down here. We're in the kitchen she shares with misery-guts upstairs. I put the bags on the floor and straighten up, flexing my fingers. She's looking at me.

Something's happened, you said. What?

It's . . . you know Ronnie? I'd hoped to approach the subject gradually, over a cup of tea or something. Not like this.

No I *don't* know Ronnie and I don't want to, but I know who he is. Is this about him?

Y . . . yes.

Well, go on.

It's hard, Gran. I'm scared you won't believe me. Mum doesn't.

Well you won't know till you try me, will you?

I suppose not. The thing is Gran, he . . . *molests* me. I think that's the word.

Ha! She nods. I won't say I'm surprised, Nikki, 'cause I'm not. I *told* your mother she was making a big mistake, told her she'd be sorry. You don't know what you're chucking away I said to her, and you don't know what you're getting in its place either. And I was right, wasn't I?

13

I nod, wishing she didn't sound so pleased about it. Yes Gran, I murmur, you were right, but Mum doesn't know that. She thinks Ronnie can do no wrong. She switched off when I tried to tell her what he does, what happened on bonfire night, why I ran out the house in just a blouse. She *saw* me like that and she *still* won't believe me.

And you haven't . . . encouraged him, I suppose? Swanning about the house half dressed, that sort of thing?

Of *course* I haven't. What d'you think I *am* Gran, a slag? I shouldn't have said that, know as soon as it's out I shouldn't, but it's too late. She shakes her head.

Slag's *daughter*, love. Not the same thing, and not your fault. Shall we have a nice cup of tea?

Nick

That cold don for us. We was bumpin along til Nowember, then com the cold and fings happen bang bang bang, like that. Firs Jack lets me go and I gotta tel Ma. She larfs, sez, don't fret Nick we manage, cut back on the venison, sell the secon carridge. Ma's that sort, see: if ther's a larf somwher, she find it. Still the odd larf abowt, erly Nowember. I sez, I get work Ma. Market mebbe, or down the docks; always takin coves on down the docks.

They wasn't tho. I gon down ther nex day, noffing. Fousand coves, no ships. Same day after, day after that. I walks the streets lookin for somfing, anyfing. My bootsoles com so fin, if I stept on a penny I feels wevver its heds or tails but ther aint no penny, jus wind off of the river, cold like a hycicle, stabbin frou my fin coat.

Cupple nites later I gets home and Ma sez, they got no more stitchin for me and Connie, Nick. She bin cryin.

Til wen, I sez, and Ma shex her hed.

Dint say: long time I reckon.

Wot dosh we got, I sez.

Penny ha'penny and half a loaf, she sez, nor she can't find the larf in it neever.

That dosh feed us free days. No banquet mind, and no coals. We got fire now same like Jimmy o'Dowd, wiv saveloys to match. Little Connie moanin, holdin herself round the middle, shivrin. Baby howlin. Ma quiet, but suffrin I can tell. My feet's bad: I stuft paper in my boots to make 'em ficker but pavement com frou after a mile or two, and I fink I'm startin to go mad, cos nex day I seen somfing wot aint ther.

I bin walkin hours arstin for work wen I seen it. Arstin, arstin and always the same anser: noffing doin son, sorry, only not half as sorry as me. Anyway it's comin dark and I'm up norf somwher by a canal, and I seen a table in the middle of the road. Long it is, and piled wiv grub, same like a picter I seen in a book at ragged school: King Henry havin a banquet. King Henry aint ther o'course, bein as how he's ded. Ther's just his table wiv his supper on it, and it's a heavy supper at that. I seen hot beef and capons and fishes and fruits and gold cups wot I spose got wine in 'em. Ther's even a pig's head wiv a happle in its mouf. I must be losin my mind, cos I never stops to wonder wot King Henry's supper mite be doin in the middle of the road, even spose he wasn't ded. I even finks I can smell the grub. Water fills my mouf and I moves tord the table, got my eye on a silvery platter wiv a fat capon on it. I'm so close to that capon I can see the little holes in its skin wher the fevvers use to be, then all at once it aint ther. Not jus the capon, the hole table and evryfing on it fades away, leaving me standin in the road wiv my hand owt and slaver freezin on my chin.

I'm scairt I can tell you, so scairt I forgets I'm hungry and *that*'s sayin somfing. I turns, starts to hurry home, tho

16

noffing waitin ther but empty bellies, empty eyes, an empty hearth. And big coves in white coats mebbe, com for me and Jimmy o'Dowd.

The wit and wisdom of Solomon Stern, sitting magistrate at the Portland Road Police Court: 29 November 1853

STERN: The officer has told this court how he observed you, Thomas Mullins, on your knees under a coster-monger's cart in Camden High Street, gathering fallen apples and hiding them in the pockets of the greatcoat you are wearing now. What have you to say to that?

MULLINS: That it's true sir, what the officer says.

STERN: So you *admit* the offence, you brazen urchin?

MULLINS: Yes sir, but I didn't know it was a hoffence. The apples was half-spoilt and lying in the snow, sir. I thought 'em throwed away.

STERN: Half-spoilt and lying, eh? An apt description of *yourself*, I think.

MULLINS: I . . . don't understand, sir.

STERN: You don't understand sir. How old are you, Mullins?

MULLINS: Thirteen, sir.

STERN: Thirteen, and you don't understand. Tell me, if you weren't aware you were committing an offence, why did you conceal the apples in your pocket?

MULLINS: Where else might I have put 'em, sir, being as I needed my hands to crawl?

STERN: Are you being insolent, boy?

MULLINS: Not a *purpose*, sir. I only means I put 'em into my pockets in order to carry 'em home, sir.

STERN: I put it to you that you hid those apples because you knew full well that what you were doing was wrong: that you were *stealing* the apples.

MULLINS: No, sir.

STERN: No? Then why did you not say to the coster-monger, *excuse me guv, might I be permitted to retrieve those half-spoilt apples I see there under your cart?*

MULLINS: Ho yes *I* should fink so. Arstin for one upside the 'ead that'd be, sir.

STERN: Why, if he'd discarded the fruit?

MULLINS: Why? I can't say sir, 'cept that's how costers is. *You* try arstin for spoilt apples, see what you gets.

STERN: *Silence*, or I'll clear the court. I will *not* have my courtroom used like a penny gaff. As for *you*, Mullins, you stand revealed as both a hardened thief *and* an ill-bred, insolent young ruffian. You will go to prison for twenty-one days.

MULLINS: But sir, I cares for my widowed mother and four sisters. They're starving and I'm their only . . .

STERN: Yes, and I suppose you also support a blind, one-legged grandmother, a dancing bear and seventeen slavering cousins but you see, you should've thought of these awesome responsibilities before you committed the offence. Take him down.

Nikki

So I'm drinking tea with my gran, who thinks my mother's a slag. I haven't leapt to Mum's defence though I know she's no slag: I have to keep Gran onside so she won't boot me out. The tea's welcome but the situation's uncomfortable.

So, she says, eyeballing me over the rim of her mug, what you going to do?

I swallow a mouthful of tea, shrug. I dunno. I'm hoping you'll let me stay here for a night or two.

Well yes, she says, you can stay a night or two but then what? I mean you're only fourteen. There's school. Your mother'll report you missing, the police'll find you, take you back. I'd go to them first if I was you. Tell 'em about Ronnie, what he's been doing to you.

No! I shake my head. I can't do that, Gran, Mum'd get into trouble as well. I thought I'd like, disappear. Get a room. A job.

Gran snorts. A *room*? Who d'you think's going to let a room to a gel your age, Nikki? And as for a *job*, there's thousands looking for work. D'you expect some fool to risk employing a runaway kid when he's hundreds of applicants to choose from? She shakes her head. No. Only one thing you can do love: split on lover-boy Ronnie and go home. It was *your* home before it was his.

I drain my mug, put it on the table. I told you Gran, I can't.

21

They'd say Mum was negligent or something, which she's not. There's got to be another way.

Gran pulls a face. If there is, I don't know of it. She looks at me. Unless . . .

What?

Well there's your dad, up in Yorkshire. He'd take you in, I'm sure.

Oh yeah, but Mum . . .

What *about* your mum? Surely she'd sooner you were with your dad than loose in London, nowhere to sleep?

I dunno. I shake my head. Mum's . . . funny about Dad. Says if he cared about us, me and Marie that is, he'd want to see us but we never hear from him, not even birthdays and Christmas.

Gran gazes at me. Your dad was badly hurt when he found out about your mother and that . . . *person* she was seeing, Nikki. That *pervert*. Takes a lot of getting over, something like that. Doesn't mean he doesn't love his kids. He tried to get custody if you remember, but the court knocked him back. I'll get him on the phone if you like.

Oh I . . . dunno, Gran. It'd feel weird, talking to him after all this time. What if he's . . . you know . . . *got* someone? A girlfriend? *She* wouldn't fancy some kid showing up I bet; kid she's never seen.

Gran smiles. Your dad *has* found somebody, Nikki. Her name's Laura. You'd like her. She's a solicitor, nicely spoken, always immaculately turned out, and absolutely *devoted* to your father. I'm sure she wouldn't mind a *bit* if his daughter turned up looking for a new mum.

New mum. I look at her. I can't believe you said that to me, Gran. I've *got* a mum, I'm not looking for another, especially some toffee-nosed solicitor who's *always immaculately turned out*.

I get up, start putting my coat on and she goes, what's up? You were never this touchy when you were small.

I don't answer. I've sussed that if I stay the old bag'll never stop slagging mum off, contrasting her with Laura the devoted solicitor who probably had posh parents and never went short of anything in her life; who took my dad away from Mum, who never had anything till she had him.

I walk out without another word, into the cold. It's dusk, coming on to rain. I start running, I don't know why: she's not coming after me. I go down some steps on to the towpath of the Regent's Canal, black water pocked with rain. I jog, my bag bumping my leg till I come to a ramp. I slow to a walk up the ramp, which leads to the High Street. I start to cross and then I notice this lad on the pavement, watching me. It's nearly dark but I sense there's something not quite right about him: it's his kit, or maybe his hair. Probably one of these nutters you run into sometimes, talking to themselves or shouting abuse. Anyway I'm heading straight for him so I alter course, avoiding eye contact, and when I look again he's gone.

Nick

No big coves in white coats fank god, but Jimmy o'Dowd sittin on the floor in his room eatin sossidges wot aint ther. I looks in. Evenin Jimmy, I sez, I seen a capon jus like them sossidges.

He glares up at me, face twitchin like a killt rabbit. How can a capon be like sossidges, he sez. You *darft*, Nick Webley, witch it's wot I'm scairt of so wisht I never said it.

Ma sitting on the floor same like Mad Jimmy, rockin Fan. Fan screemin, little legs kickin under her fin raggy shawl. Wher's the chair, I sez. We had one chair lef of a set Father made. Ma nods to the hearth. I fink she burnt Father's chair, then I seen this broken loaf on a bit of cloff.

I solt that chair to buy bread, she sez.

Father's last chair, I sez.

She rocks Fan, shushin. Little won's starvin Nick, can't eat chairs. Any luck?

I shex my hed. Noffing, Ma. Wher's Connie?

Ma's cryin sofly, not loud like little Fan. Connie holdin horses heds, she sez.

She's too little for that job, I sez. Horses wery strong, Ma.

Ma nods. I know, but at least she's got good bread inside her, Nick. Eat some yorself, you mus be famisht.

Wot abowt you, I sez.

I had mine she sez, but I don't fink so.

Lot left, I sez, lookin at her. She's fiddlin wiv Fan, makin her snugger, only not wery snug cos shawl so fin.

Big loaf, she sez wivowt lookin at me, and it should be. Cost me my Daniel's chair. She's like to choke wiv cryin.

I knows she's not et but too hungry to argue. I sits down crossleg, tears chunks off of this loaf, stuffs 'em in my mouf. Taste like necter. I dunno wot is this necter, but you hear coves say this taste like necter, that taste like necter: happles, beer, anyfing. I fink necter wot angels eats in heaven, so Father eatin it now.

Nick, sez Ma. Fan's took a little bread in water and went off at last.

Wot is it Ma, I sez. I'm finished eatin, tho not full up. Hole in my middle not full if I swaller Sent Pauls.

I bin finkin abowt the workhouse, she sez.

My belly goes cold like snow. No Ma, I sez. No Webleys *never* went to the workhouse.

Nick, she sez, we done our best. Solt *evryfing* 'cept our boots and cloves. Look at us: we sits on bare boards, sleeps on 'em. They got beds at the workhouse, chairs. They got wittles as well, witch it's more than we got mos the time. I can't watch my little wons pine, Nick. Workhouse better'n that. Fambly acrost the way – Missus Mullins and her gels – they gon today.

I looks at her. Wait free days, I sez. I find somfing, I *promise*. I'm pullin soggy paper owt my boots, won got a hole frou. She nods at it. Boots fallin to bits Nick. You can't go barefoot in the snow.

Vy not, I sez, there's plenty as *does*. Bare arse and all com to that. Free days, Ma.

Free, she sez, Fan twistin in her arms. Free days, Nick. If noffing com then I take my babies, ring the workhouse bell.

I don't say noffing. I'm done in. I finds a dry bit of floor, stretches owt but sleep don't com. I got the workhouse inside my hed, and Connie, holding freezin reins wiv frozen hands.

Nikki

The rain gets heavier. I'm passing Camden tube station so I duck into the entrance. There's a tall guy selling the *Big Issue*. He grins at me. Bloody English weather, eh?

I nod, putting my bag down so I can peel off my jacket. It's supposed to be showerproof but my jumper's damp on the shoulders and sleeves and it's gone through my shirt too. Look at this, I growl, plucking up a bit of sleeve. Showerproof they call it: wouldn't keep gnat piss out.

He laughs. I can tell he's startled by my language. All lies darling, adverts. Except in here o'course. Holding out his wodge of magazines.

I realize he wants me to buy a copy, but I have to be careful with my dosh. I smile, apologetic. Sorry, I'm a bit short just now. His eyes tell me he doesn't believe me and why should he. I don't *look* poor, and it's probably what everybody says. Guilt loosens my tongue. I . . . left home, I tell him. Today. I haven't found a room yet.

A room? He frowns, shakes his head. You won't find one now love. It's nearly six. How old are you, if you don't mind me asking?

Fourteen.

Fourteen? He pulls a face. I was going to suggest you try one of the hostels – Centrepoint, Shelter – but they're obliged to tell the law if you're under sixteen.

No! I shake my head. Police'd take me back. I can't go back.

They'd let you stay tonight, couple of nights mebbe, before . . .

No, no way. Don't want to take the chance.

He shrugs. Better'n skippering in a doorway darling, but it's your life. He looks at me. Never tried it have you?

What?

Sleeping rough.

I shake my head. No, but . . .

'S no fun, trust me, specially now winter's coming on. Don't you have a rellie you could go to? Auntie or sommink?

No.

Well look, don't take this the wrong way, but there's a sofa doing nothing in my flat. You could . . . you know, just for tonight.

Oh yeah, like I *would*.

No, listen. His expression is earnest. I know what it sounds like and I don't blame you: I'd be suspicious if I was a gel but you see . . . He glances about him, lowers his voice. I'm er . . . *immune* to feminine charms, know what I'm saying?

I . . . think so, yes.

Good, 'cause what that means is, you'll get no hassle from me. What you *will* get, if you decide to take me up on my fantastic offer, is a bite to eat and a safe, comfy bed for the night. Spot of breakfast as well, if you're lucky.

And you, I ask. What will *you* get?

Me? He shrugs again, grins. Company I suppose, and not having to lie awake all night thinking of you huddled in some doorway, shivering.

Is that what you'd do? If I didn't come, I mean.

Certainly.

Why? I'm not your problem. You're not responsible for me.

He smiles. He's got a seriously cute smile. Some of us believe everybody's responsible for everybody else, he says. He sounds so nice when he says this, so *sincere*, that I feel ready to follow him anywhere and so I accept his offer.

I know: serial killers probably sound exactly like that.

Nick

Connie com in wery late, cold and wet. She holded four horses for free halfpence. Ma let a penny candle burn til she com home, so my sister workit half the nite for a halfpenny. Ma rubs her dry wiv rags, I warms a cup of water little bit little bit over that candle, breaks bits of bread in, witch it's not soup but *like* soup if you hungry enuff. Our commotion wakes Fan, who screems til Connie dips a rag in her supper, pokes it in babby's mouf. Only water, but babby finks she's suckin milk and soon sleepin, or startin to die mebbe. We lies on the floor and shuts our eyes, Ma, Connie and me. Wind boomin in the cold chimny, roof creeks wiv weight of snow on it and Jimmy o'Dowd weepin in his smelly room. One part of me wants to sleep forever, ovver part wants morning to com quick quick.

Mebbe I go see my old gaffer Jack tomorrer. Jus to say hallo.

Nikki

He's called Steve Patten and he lives in Bermondsey. He knocks off at six, four copies of the magazine unsold, and we ride the tube to London Bridge. It's completely dark when we get there. We set off walking in the rain.

How far is it?

Balaclava Road. Not far.

He's got long legs and I'm trotting to keep up. I'm not completely stupid so I feel a bit nervous. Well, I don't know this part of London at all and I don't know *him*. I've got seventy quid on me: guys've killed for less. He seems nice, but so does Ronnie to people who don't know him. I'm psyching myself up to say sorry, I made a mistake, when he turns through a gateway. Here we are Nikki, he says, soon have you warm and dry.

He uses a latchkey to let us into a dim hallway. I'm upstairs, he tells me, and I follow him up a creaky flight thinking: is this my last walk; will they carry me down in a bodybag? At the top he uses another key and I step into his flat. He follows me in and shuts the door and that's it. Whatever happens now, happens. He flicks a light-switch, sees the look on my face and reads my mind. No darling, he laughs. I'm *not* a psychopathic killer. I don't lure little girls here to throttle them and arrange their corpses under the floorboards like a stamp collection, so relax and I'll show you where everything is, okay?

It's tiny. Sitting room, bedroom, bathroom with toilet. One of those old-fashioned, high-ceilinged places that can be really grotty and usually are, but Steve keeps this one immaculate. Dustfree surfaces, no bits on the carpet, even the bathroom smells fresh. I'm reassured enough to smile and say, hmmm, nice.

He's pleased, I can tell. Glad you like it. He smiles ruefully. One snag: I share a kitchen with downstairs, so why don't I go fix us something to eat while you wash and change? He grins. There's a bolt on the bathroom door, you'll be completely private. Have a bath if you like. He looks at my bag. You do *have* a change of kit, don't you?

I nod. Yes.

Good, because in spite of what some people may think I *don*'t keep women's clothes to mince around in when the fancy takes me.

I know that, Steve. I'm not one of those thickos. I feel myself blush.

He grins, changes the subject. Pasta suit you?

Huh? Oh yeah, lovely.

He goes downstairs, I take my bag to the bathroom. There is a bolt and I slide it home, which makes me feel ungrateful somehow. I decide I won't have a bath: heating water's expensive and dosh must be tight. I make do with the tiny handbasin, stuff my laundry in my bag. I'm brushing my hair when I hear him return.

Nick

Morning coms pretty quick at that, wiv me as tired as wen I lays down, and colder. I finks, this day number won of the free Ma giv me befor she rings that workhouse bell, but this fink don't stop me doin somfing darft.

Wot I done is, I starts finkin abowt gamblin, or *tossin*. Costers loves to toss the coins. I seen a cove won time start wiv a flatch, witch means a halfpenny, and walk away wiv a couter, witch is a sovereign. Earnt it pretty quick and all, quicker'n workin. So I gets this in my hed and it won't go away so wot do I do? I tels Ma I'm off to look for work but goes down by the river wher tossin goes on. I hopes to win, carry a couter back to Ma, but I knowd from the start I didn't ought to've went. It's colder'n ever, speshly by the river wher wind blowin and water froze rite acrost, but it takes more'n cold to stop costers gamblin, so not long til I finds men behind a old boat, tossin. Agin the law that gamblin, witch is why they're behind a boat wher Peelers can't spy 'em.

I got no money to play wiv so wot I does is, I scouts. Scout means keep a lookout for the hofficers, holler if won's comin. Little lads scouts, but this big lad needs the halfpence so I scouts til twelve witch it's dinnertime, gets owl-yenep witch means tuppence. If only I *kep* that tuppence, took it home to Ma, everyfing fine. Bread *and* tea, tuppence'll buy, but I dint. I dint. Wot I done is join in the tossin and I has bad luck and soon that tuppence like Jimmy o'Dowd saveloys: not there. Now I got noffing, witch it's wot I come wiv, but that workhouse won day closer for Ma and my little sisters.

I can't go home, can't tel Ma wot I done. I hurrys about, lookin in butchers and fat-boilers and catsmeat shops, arstin any work, any work, but nobody wantin a lad, speshly now dark coming on. There's danger in the dark: sneaks, dog-thieves, thieves wot rolls drunks, them as takes from nippers, and bad women such as child-strippers and unforchnate women and soldiers' women and the coves wot pertects 'em. Streets round Sharp's Rents is fronged wiv bad peeple, a cove gotta mind hisself evry minnit. I'm freezing, feets wet inside them holy boots and hungry too. I wants to go home but not wivowt money, not wivowt a halfpenny even, so at last I walks by Jack's pitch. I tels myself it's jus to say hulloa, but reely I hopes Jack'll give me somfing.

Nick, he sez, wen he clapt eyes on me. Nick my poor fellow, you looks done in. Jack's cart just abowt bare and he's finner'n I ever seen him, but I'm so desperate I tells him the little gels starving and Ma too. I'm ashamed: Webleys never bin beggars but I can't go home empty handed. Oh Nick, sez Jack, I got no dosh to giv, fings so hard but here, tek these. And he push four happles in my pocket.

I looks at him. Jack, I sez, wen this cold gon I'll nipper for you til these happles paid for.

Don't tork darft boy, he sez, wot's four happles. Go

34

home, he sez, owt of this wind, tel your movver Jack and Bet finks of her.

Walkin home I done anovver darft fing: I pops my jacket. *Pops* is wen you borrers a few coppers off a pornshop and the cove makes you leave somfing wiv him, somfing worf more'n he's lended o'course. You spose to com back anovver day, pay back the coppers and a bit more, get the fing you left, only mos peeple don't com back cos they never has the money, so the cove sels the fings they popped. I don't spec to see my jacket agen but not finking abowt that; finking abowt comin home wiv bread and hot pies and happles for Ma and the little gels, seein their faces.

Hallo little wons. See wot yor mad brovver got for you.

Nikki

All right? he smiles as I come out the bathroom. He's holding a pan of red sauce in one hand, a plastic ladle in the other. On the table are two dinner plates heaped with steaming spaghetti.

I smile back. Lovely, thanks. Just what I needed. I nod at the food. That looks good too.

He grins. Probably looks better than it is but still, it'll stop us starving to death in the night. Have a seat.

He ladles sauce on my pasta, then on his. My own recipe, he says. Tinned tomatoes and tuna. I call it Pasta Joke. He sits down opposite, slides a wooden peppermill across.

I screw black pepper on my food, push the mill his way. Comfy setup you've got, Steve. Peppermill and everything.

For a *Big Issue* vendor, you mean.

No, I didn't say . . .

It's all right Nikki, I *do* have a comfy setup. It's not typical. I'm lucky, I've got generous friends.

You're a generous friend yourself.

He shrugs. Like I told you, some of us think we're all responsible for one another. Did you spot the line, by the way?

Huh?

Washline, over the bath. Thin items guaranteed to dry overnight.

No. I shake my head. I didn't notice it. I wouldn't mind . . .

Fine. He smiles. After dinner, eh?

I'm chasing a last strand of spaghetti with my fork when he says, no pudding I'm afraid.

I shake my head. Couldn't manage any if there was, I'm pogged. And it *was* as good as it looked.

Cheers, glad you enjoyed it. He stands up. I'll go wash up while you use the magic clothesline.

No, I'll come with you, wipe.

No need, and no room in the kitchen for two anyway. I'll only be a tick, then we can sit and listen to the latest sounds around. There's no TV.

Latest sounds. He tunes his radio to channel one and we listen till eleven, talking whenever they play something naff which is pretty often. Steve's really nice and I enjoy the evening more than I'd expected. At eleven he yawns and says, I don't know about you Nikki, but I'm knackered. He smiles. I've had second thoughts about that sofa you're sitting on. *I'm* taking it and you can have the bed, as long as you don't mind sleeping in my sheets.

I start to protest but he insists, fetching a blanket and pillow from the bedroom and dropping them on the sofa, which doesn't look long enough for him. I'll be fine, he says when I mention this. He nods towards the bedroom door and says, you'll find there's a bolt on that one as well. Good night, Nikki. Sleep tight.

I don't shoot the bolt and I sleep like a log.

Nick

You ought to've seen little Connie wen she sniffs them pies. She coms wiv eyes like lamps, mouf waterin, little hands reechin. I'm cold like a hycicle but worf it jus to see 'er like that. Hot, I sez, larfin, tippin a pie into her hands but she don't mind hot. Better'n cold. I watch her sit on the floor, crammin her little mouf, feel warm in my hart.

Here Ma. Ma's in her corner lookin at me. I holds owt pies for her and Fan but she don't take 'em, sez, wher's your jacket Nick.

Popt it, Ma.

You *wot*, boy.

Popt it, I sez. Little wons hungry, can't eat cloff no more'n chairs.

Fool, she sez. How you gonna look for work wiv holy boots and no jacket.

Hard Ma, I sez, that's how I'm gonna look. Two more days.

Aye. She nods. But spose you goes owt tomorrer morning and never coms back, cold gotcha: wot'll becom of your sisters *then*, eh.

I looks at her hard. That's wen you takes 'em to that workhouse, Ma: *over my ded body*. Here. I offers the pies, witch them free parts cold by now.

Wher's yors, she sez.

Et it comin along, I sez, witch it's the troof.

She looks at me a minnit, takes the pies, sits down by Fan. Fan's too little to eat her pie: mos of it goes on her face and the floor. Ma helps her, breakin off bits to push in babby's mouf, eatin her own between. I leans on the wall, hands in pockets, watch my fambly fill their belly, finkin, Father lookin down, seen somfing good for once. I sez to Father inside my head: I won't see 'em in the work-house Father, I swears. I'll do anyfing, *anyfing* afore that. No Webley's ever went to the workhouse, nor never will.

Somfing good com tomorrer, cos a hoaf sweard on a ded father's a parful fing, innit?

Nikki

He knocks at seven, calls through the door. Sorry Nikki: gotta be out by eight, collect my papers. I'm down the kitchen for a bit.

Swinging my feet to the threadbare carpet I think, what a sweetie: lets me know I'm alone so I can head for the bathroom without a dressing-gown. I grab my clothes and hairbrush and scurry through, feeling vulnerable anyway. He was right about the washline: my bits and pieces're completely dry. I wash, dress, brush my hair and carry my laundry back to the bedroom. I'm zipping up my bag when I hear him return.

Morning Steve. There's a plate of toasted bagels and two mugs of steaming instant on the table.

He smiles. Morning Nikki. Sleep okay?

Yes thanks. How about you?

Fine. Come and eat.

I sit, take a bagel, look for butter. There's a heap of those little foil packets you get in cafes.

Steve is apologetic. Nicked I'm afraid. Dosh don't run to butter by the slab. Sugar comes the same way. He nods towards a saucerful of paper sachets.

'S okay, I don't take sugar.

He grins. I do, if they leave it lying around.

We eat our bagels, slurp coffee. I catch his eye. It was really nice of you to let me stay, Steve. I don't know what I'd have done if you hadn't.

He shakes his head. It was nothing, darling. What's the plan for today?

Oh: keep looking for that room, I suppose. And a job.

He pulls a face. Long shots love, both of 'em. Look. He drains his mug, sets it down. Why don't you consider this your base, eh? Look for work, look for a place, come back here at night till you've found sommink.

No. I shake my head. It's lovely of you Steve and it's very, very tempting, but I've got to learn to make it by myself. I know if I don't, I'll end up crawling back to my gran or even home.

He gazes at me across the table. I don't usually ask people this, Nikki, and it'll serve me right if you tell me to mind my own business, but why'd you leave home, and what'd be so terrible about going back?

So I tell him about Ronnie. Hadn't planned to, hate talking about it, but Steve's been so good to me I feel I owe him. He listens gravely, shakes his head when I've finished. Y'know, you could get *him* kicked out, Nikki. Courts'd slap a whatsit on him, restraining order, not to come within five hundred yards of your mum's house. 'T ain't fair *you*'ve got to be homeless because he can't keep his hands to himself.

I nod. I know Steve, but he's Mum's partner. She's crazy about him, I can't be the cause of them splitting up. And anyway, all that court stuff, the police. I thought about it before I walked out and I'm sure it's for the best.

He pulls a face. Well, like I said last night it's your life, but at least keep a note of the address so if things get . . . you know, too heavy, you've got a crashpad. Yeah?

He writes the address on a bit of paper and makes me put it in my bag, then leads me downstairs and out to the pavement.

He's going south, I'm off north. He wishes me luck and we walk away from each other, and I can't help feeling I've turned down something good.

Nick

Somfing good tomorrer. Somfing bad firs tho: snow on strong wind witch scholards calls a *blizzard*. Jus wot a cove don't want who popt his jacket. I raps my arms rownd my middle and tramps wiv my hed down arstin, arstin same like ovver days and same anser too: no boys wanted. Dinnertime my feets ded wiv cold and the rest of me soon to foller I reckons. A Webley never frows in the towel but I'm cryin a bit, I admits. I'm so cold I stops seekin work to look for a brazier, but no work, no brazier, no luck.

I'm not a thief nor never was, but wot happens next makes me a thief and I can't help it. It comes out like this: I'm trampin half-faintin on Silver Street looking for a warm wen I seen the bake potato man. Bake potato man got this tin oven wiv legs witch it got hot coals in won part and hot water in won part and bake potatoes in anovver part. I goes up to him: no halfpenny so no potato but I hopes he seen blue skin frou my wet shirt, let me stand by that oven a bit to save my life, but straitaway fings goes rong. Bake potato man got little dog tied to an oven leg, witch it starts to yap and leep abowt ven it seen me. Finks it seen a ded man walkin, probly. Bake potato man curses, kicks owt and that little dog takes off same like I would, sombody kickin me. Tin oven's jerked off its legs, topples over and spills red coals sizzlin on the slush and steamy water and hot potatoes rollin all abowt. Little dog afraid wot he done, tries to run, drags that oven acrost the snow. Bake potato man goes cursin after him and in a trice ther's coves evrywher, wimmin and nippers too, snatchin up them hot potatoes and makin off. I finks . . . no I *doesn*'t fink: I jus grabs won potato and runs, same like that little dog 'cept quicker. I pelts along Silver Street, swerves right up Great Pulteney Street and scuds up a court hentry. Courts is mosly dark and filfy so Peelers avoids 'em if they can; they prefers to see a thief in a different sort of court, so I'm safe. I sits down on a snowy step and starts to scoff that potato. Peeler *does* happen to fancy his boots dirty, its prison for me or Bot'ny Bay, but I'm so hungry I don't care. Only fing as matters is the lovely heat off that potato warmin hands and mouf and belly all at once.

Then a door opens at my back and I turns and sees a toff lookin down at me.

Nikki

Useless, useless day. Camden, Paddington, King's Cross, Swiss Cottage: you name it, I've walked it, and all for nothing. No room, no job. I'm beginning to realize I really didn't know what I was taking on when I ran away from home. Steve told me of course: long shots both of 'em, he said, and he was right.

So. Can't go home, can't crawl back to Gran's, won't sponge on Steve. By lunchtime I know I'm looking at sleeping out. What does Steve call it: skippering? Sounds like the sea doesn't it; there's a hint of fish. Well that's me. All at sea, a fish out of water. I mean you see 'em, the homeless, see 'em everywhere, and you know a lot of them sleep rough but you never bother to wonder *how*. How do you choose your spot, and what do you need? I've seen 'em in sleeping bags but I haven't got one. Rolled up in blankets like a cocoon, but I didn't bring a blanket either. There I was packing my bag, congratulating myself on not forgetting anything: change of kit, clean underwear, hairbrush, toothbrush, sweater, second pair of shoes, nail-clippers. *Nail-clippers* for God's sake: absolutely crucial when you're huddled in some doorway on a freezing December night.

Yes, it's December. Wednesday the nineteenth to be precise. Six more shopping days to Christmas. Oxford Street and Regent Street'll look gorgeous tonight, all tinsel and coloured lights. Not that I've ever shopped in Oxford Street. I *wish*, but joining the crowds gawping through sparkling plate-glass windows at all those arty, cute and cosy seasonal tableaux has been a delicious prelude to Christmas for me since I was a little kid. Bet it doesn't feel quite the same though, when you've no bed to go home to, no fat bird in the fridge, no chimney for Santa to squeeze down. Funny how stuff like that never occurs to you till you're in the situation yourself.

Only bright bit of the day comes at half-twelve when I call Kirsty. She must've been waiting because she answers in a flash.

That you, Nikki?

No, it's Victoria Beckham.

Where *are* you? Your mum come round last night, crying. I felt awful.

You didn't *tell* her anything?

No, but I *wanted* to. She asked if you'd phoned and I don't think she believed me when I said no because she showed up at school this morning: Old Baker sent for me and there she was in his office and *he* asked me.

Just you?

No, he got Janice and Daisy and Philippa in as well, but *they* didn't have to lie. Why can't I say I've talked to you, Nikki? She wouldn't know where you called from, and at least she'd know you haven't been murdered or something.

Is that what she thinks?

Course. First thing *anybody*'d think, isn't it?

I dunno. Kids run off all the time, but listen; *tell* her if you think it's best. You needn't say you lied. Tell her I called today. Say I'm safe and well, but I'm not coming back because what I told her's true and she won't believe me.

What *did* you tell her, Nikki?

46

Oh, it was about Ronnie, I don't want to go into it. Can you remember what to say?

You're not coming back because what you told her's true and she wouldn't believe you.

Right.

Can I meet you somewhere, Nikki? We break up this afternoon, I could come tomorrow.

No. I mean it'd be great to see you, but it'd make it harder for me to stay away. I can't explain.

It's okay then. Just don't stop calling.

I won't, course I won't. It makes my day, talking to you. Don't think I've gone off you Kirsty, just because I won't let us meet up. You're even more important to me now. My only link to the real world if you know what I mean.

Yeah, I think I do, and I'll be here for you, I promise.

I know you will, Kirsty. You're the best mate anybody ever had.

Hey. You're not *crying* are you?

Course not. *Would* I? I'm gonna ring off now though, save my free minutes.

Save 'em? You'd three hundred and forty last week, you spack.

Yeah, well. Same time tomorrow?

Look forward to it. I'll call your mum, and you look after yourself, okay? Don't wander about by yourself after dark.

No I won't. Bye Kirsty.

Who'm I gonna wander about with, I wonder: Lara Croft?

Nick

Hullo my fine fellow, sez the toff on the top step. I jumps up, crams the last bit of potato in my mouf and sprays most of it owt again tryin to give him a Good Day. I finks he probly fetch the constable, giv me in charge but mebbe not if I coms the young gentleman. Good Day sir, I splutters.

He looks me up and down. Are you presently engaged? he sez in his toff voice.

Wot, I sez.

He blows out his breff like a cab horse. Are you in a *situation*, fellow? Gainfully employed? Snowflakes fallin on his coat, he brushes 'em off. I finks mebbe he don't mean to turn me in after all.

Sitivation, I sez. O yessir, I'm in a sitivation: sitivation of cold wet and hungry, Ma and sisters to support but not gainfully hemployed at the present, fank you for arstin.

He larfs. *I*'d larf, fick coat on, warm room at my back.

Then you're free to perform a small service for me, he sez.

Yessir, I sez, finkin, wot service.

Splendid. He makes a half-turn, indicates the door. Step into the lobby if you please.

If I please. I'm frou that door like a rat down a cesspit, hart bumpin cos here's work, nor I wasn't even *arstin*.

Lobby's a dim place, doors boaf sides. Toff goes frou won door, I stands drippin. Warm here so I don't care if he never coms back but he does, bit of paper in his hand. Do you know the apothecary in Marshall Street?

Yes sir, I sez. I don't know no pothecry in Marshall Street cos I never heard of Marshall Street but I got a tong in my head, I can arst.

Splendid. That's how he speek: splendid. Hand the apothecary this note, wait for the parcel he'll make up, bring it here and I'll give you a penny. He smiles. Be back in fifteen minutes and I'll give you sixpence.

Sixpence. Ma and the little wons eat two days off of that sixpence. I nods. I'll be back in *fourteen* minutes sir, I sez, and he larfs. I tucks his note inside my shirt, goes owt. I'm wet frou and feet sore, but that sixpence same like cabman's whip to me. I trots.

Doctor Snow's boy eh? sez the pothecry wen I givs him the note.

I shakes my head. Don't know the gentleman's name sir, but he teld me be quick.

He larfs, sez, don't fret yourself boy, I'll not keep you dripping on my floor any longer than I must. He fusses abowt, I looks at all his bottles witch they got funny writin on like TINCT. MYRRH. Don't mean noffing if you arst me, Tinct Myrrh.

Wen he done the parcel I sez, how long I bin waitin sir.

He larfs again. The Larfing Pothecry, I finks, twice nightly at the Vic. No longer than six minutes, he sez. Six. I sticks the parcel in my shirt and hurries owt.

Fifteen and a half minutes, sez Doctor Snow, big gold watch in his hand. No sixpence, I finks, but a penny's better'n noffing. My face probly glum tho cos he sez, no sulking sir, I'll not gull you. Fifteen and a half minutes over treacherous ice is most commendable. You shall have your sixpence.

See: a hoaf sweard on a ded father's a parful fing.

Nikki

I don't give up after lunch. I knock at a house or two where there's cards in the window but my heart's not in it and I get the usual response. One old dear looks at me through watery eyes and quavers, *go home dear, it's Christmas*. Like I don't know. Half of me's keeping an eye open for skippering spots, and if you think that's not seriously scary you've never had to do it. I find myself thinking about Kirsty and the others at school, last day, can't wait for it to be half-three so they can ride home to where the festivities're waiting to start because you see, that old dear was right: it's all about home, Christmas is. It's a family thing, more so than other holidays really. I read once that more lonely people commit suicide at Christmas than any other time. It didn't make much impression when I read it, but you can bet it's starting to make sense now.

The light's going. I look at my watch and it's four-ten. School let out forty minutes ago and I didn't even notice. All my friends'll be home by now except Philippa, and she'll be on the train. Lives in a place called Pratt's Bottom, old Pippa does, and gets a lot of stick for it, but her bottom'll rest comfier tonight than *this* prat's bottom will, for sure.

It's getting busier because everybody's leaving work, heading for the tube, the trains. I'm on Euston Road by the British Library and people're streaming past. They've all got destinations except me. Places to go. Familiar places, familiar faces. Is the word familiar related to family? Never thought of that before. Never thought of a lot of things before. Soon all these people with places to go will have gone to them, leaving the streets to those who aren't going anywhere because it doesn't matter where they go: they have no appointments to keep. Nobody's expecting them. All places are the same to people like that.

People like me.

Nick

A parful fing, nor it aint done wiv me yet. The Doctor fishes in his pocket, gives me a sixpence. I sez, fank you sir, and turns to go.

Wait, he sez, you seem a bright young fellow.

I makes him a little bow. Nicholas Webley sir, I sez. My father was Daniel Webley the carpenter.

Was?

He fell off of a roof sir, past away.

I'm sorry. You mentioned a mother, sisters.

Yessir. Two sisters, Connie and Fan. This coin put wittles in 'em, save their little lifes, fank you sir.

I'm not fishing for gratitude, he sez. Would you be interested in a position?

Wotcha mean sir, position.

He blows like a cab horse again. A situation, he sez. I'm offering you a place, lad. A post. A position with regular wages. Would you like to *serve* here: join my household?

I can't bleev my ruddy ears. My hart bangs abowt like a crow in a cage. I would sir, I sez. *Indeed* I would. My voice comes owt croaky, same like that crow.

Splendid. He looks at me, frowns. Those clothes will have to go, he sez. Can't have a scarecrow hurrying about town with doctor's messages. You've nothing else, I suppose?

I shakes my hed. No sir. Evryfing solt to buy bread.

Hmmm, well . . . He finks for a minnit. Step this way, he sez. Perhaps we'll find something back here that'll fit you.

Back here's a room bigger'n ours at Sharp's Rents, and dryer. Wery dim, and so full of fings it look like the back room at a fence shop. A *fence* is a cove wot buys stuff off of thiefs so I don't say this, just finks it. Ther's beds and tables and chairs and wash-tubs and fings I dunno wot they for. And cloves. I never seen so much cloves. Cloves in chests, trunks, presses. On backs of chairs. Piled on the *floor*, same like Jimmy o'Dowd's room.

Doctor Snow seen me lookin. These premises belonged to a patient of mine, he sez, now deceased. The premises *and* their contents he left to me in settlement of fees outstanding.

Doctor Snow goes frou the room, picks up this and that, armful of cloves. Get out of those sodden rags boy, he sez, try these for size.

You can wager I done wot he sez, quick as a flash. In no time at all I'm inside of a fine fick shirt, wool trousers, wool hose. I finds a jacket as well, and a greatcoat so long it just abowt sweeps the floor.

Looks better, sez the Doctor. Feels better too I suppose.

He spose rite. I'm warm and dry, firs time since Jack turns me off. Yes fank you sir, I sez.

It's no great matter Nicholas, he sez. I'll look to see you at seven tomorrow morning.

I'll be here sir, I sez.

Not without boots, lad. He larfs at me lookin like a toff on top, bare feets below. You'll find a fit among those, I fancy. Nods to a corner wher I seen a heep of old boots, then takes hisself off. I roots abowt in them trotter-cases, tries a cuppla pair till I gets a fit. I'm lacin up wen he coms back. Oh, he sez, and if you see anything which might be suitable for your mother and those two sisters of yours, feel free to take it along.

Sootable. Christmas in four days but coms *now* for me. I sorts frou them cloves like a dog frou a bone-heep. Doctor takes hisself off agen. Soon I got so much cloves my arms won't hardly go round 'em and pocketsful and all. I goes owt to the lobby, nor I can't hardly see in front of me neever. Doctor Snow coms owt of anovver room, starts to larf. D'you want me to hire a *donkey*-cart, Nicholas?

My hart drops, he finks I've took too much. Is this too much sir, I sez.

No lad, he sez, indeed it is not. I was making a jest at your expense, that's all. Here, let me open the door.

If I looks like a ball of cloves on legs I don't care. I'm finkin abowt them little gels' faces wen they seen the warm fings I got for 'em. Ma too. *And* I got a sitivation.

As the scholard sez, my cup run a fover.

Nikki

Six o'clock I'm on Marylebone Road, dawdling, looking for a place to spend the night. It's far too early of course. If I settle down now I'll be chilled to the bone by ten o'clock and my bum'll be painful from sitting on stone, but I don't know this yet. It's one of hundreds of things I'll have to learn if I'm going to survive on the street. I list some of them in my head to keep from thinking about Steve's nice flat.

Where d'you get a cardboard box? Lots of skipperers sleep in them, but where do they *find* them?

How can you keep clean? I mean, you'd wash your hands and face in a public lavatory and I suppose you could brush your teeth, but what about the rest of you? What about washing your *hair*? You'd probably get away with rinsing a pair of knickers through, but how the heck would you get them dry?

In the middle of the night when the lavs are shut, where do you pee?

What if it's your time of the month and you're flat broke and you haven't got . . . you know?

What if a policemen asks how *old* you are?

I'm on Park Crescent now. It's nearly seven and there's loads of people about. I'm glad they're there, it feels safe, but a part of me's impatient for the night to begin. I know it's going to be awful and I want to find out *how* awful. I need to know if I can do it.

I'm peckish. They'll have finished tea an hour ago at home. Wednesday, pizzas and chips. Fries, Ronnie calls them. He's one of those people who like to use Americanisms. Fries. Bottom line. To go. Here's one that might've been *made* for you Ronnie: asshole.

I've got dosh, best part of seventy quid. No need to starve just yet. I speed up, keeping my eyes skinned for a McDonalds. Yes I *know* it's junk, but I've heard it called comfort food too and I need comfort, okay? *What if you need comfort and you've no dosh?* Shaddap!

I find one on the corner of Regent and Little Portland. It's busy: a slow fast food outlet but, hey, why'm *I* in a rush? I queue, or *stand in line* as Ronnie would say, get a cheese-burger and chips, a coke you could swim across and, miracle of miracles, I find a table.

I sit there chewing and my mind goes, *cardboard box, wonder if they get 'em here, if they'd let me have one? I could ask, but what if they ask what I want it for?*

I intend to sleep in it.

No, couldn't say that. Not yet. I am one of the homeless: just don't feel like one that's all. I could say I'm moving, want it to pack books in.

All the time this is going on inside my head I *know* I won't ask, even though I suspect I'll wish I had before the night's out. I slurp coke, watching the normal people. Some have been doing their Christmas shopping, they've got bags and parcels to find a place for and keep an eye on. Normal people. None of *them* needs a cardboard box or a deep doorway or their real dad to come back. None of them'll walk past this place when it's locked up and dark and silent.

I hog the table as long as I dare then shoot my rubbish into the bin, use the toilet and leave.

Nick

See Ma, I larfs, totterin in behind all them cloves. I spec she be happy, serprise and happy, but she aint. Oh Nick, wot you *done*, she sez, all breffy wiv fear.

I dumps them cloves on a dry bit of floor. Snow bin the ruin of us Ma, I sez, and Snow's our salvation. I finkt up this speech comin along.

Wot's it *mean* Nick, sez Ma, all this abowt snow.

I larfs. *Doctor* Snow, I tells her. All this com from Doctor Snow.

Ma's face coms white. You stealt off of a *doctor*, Nick. She looks to the door, holdin little Fan to her. Peelers com any minnit Nick, she sez. You'll get sent to the hulks. Hulks is rotten old ships they keeps coves in wot's bound for Botny Bay.

No Ma, I larfs. I dint steal the cloves, Doctor Snow *giv* 'em to me, giv me this too. I show her the sixpence. I ran a herrand for him and he deckt me owt like a toff and I'm to join his houseold from tomorrer.

Fan's wimperin. Ma rocks her, looks at me. Are you tellin me the troof Nick. Yor to be a *Doctor*'s boy.

Yes Ma, I sez.

She swallers, looks at the cloves. And these. All these are for us, from the gentleman hisself.

Yes Ma.

Oh Nick! She bleev me at last, falls to weepin. Fan fink somfing bad and starts bawlin.

No workhouse Ma, I sez. Not tomorrer, nor never. I'm cryin too, just a bit. Father done it, I sez.

Ma looks at me. Wot you mean Nick, she wispers. Your father's *ded*.

I sweard a hoaf on him Ma, I sez. On father. I sweard you never be in that workhouse, you nor his little gels. I swears that hoaf, and nex day *this*. I points to the cloves. Try somfing on, Ma, swaddle little Fan. Wher's Connie.

Ma nods to the door. Minding Missus Plowman's little wons. Missus Plowman wisiting Mister Plowman at Tothill Fields. That Tothill Fields is the house of correction wher Mister Plowman doin free month for easin a yokel of a fimble witch means, pincht his watch. Mister Plowman aint a reglar thief but got six little moufs to feed and won big mouf on Missus Plowman. I sez go fetch her Ma, soon as yor deckt out. Fetch them six little Plowmans as well wile I pops down the pie shop.

Wen I coms back wiv the wittles, pies and potatoes, bread and tea and milk, evrybody ther. Ma and Connie lookin fat in all them cloves, Fan, snug at last, sleepin, little Plowmans fin but lively, grabbin hot pies, burnin tiny fingers but don't care. We puts on our wery own *hyce-festival*, like them toffs puts on in the middle of the frozen Thames.

Shame Doctor Snow aint here to see wot a diffrence he made wiv sixpence and a pile of old cloves.

Nikki

I've found this doorway up a narrow street called Barr Street. If I bend forward and look left I can see people passing on Oxford Street. It's a quarter to eleven and they're still going past. I know it's nearly Christmas but surely the shops're shut by now?

It's dark here, that's why I chose it. It'd be less scary in a well-lit spot but I don't want people looking at me and anyway, it'd be just my luck for Ronnie to come by. *You don't want to kip in that draughty doorway sweetheart. Come on home and be my special Christmas cracker.*

I don't half wish I had a sleeping-bag. What I've done is, I've taken my sweater and spare clothes out of my bag and spread them on the tiles. It's got a tiled floor, this doorway. It's not quite as cold and uncomfortable as sitting on the floor itself but it nearly is, and I could do with *wearing* the sweater. I picture my drawer at home: four sweaters in there, plus some thick woollen socks and a scarf. Too late to think about that now, you plank.

I look at my watch. Jeez: only flipping *ten*-to. Can't believe I looked five minutes ago: feels like half an hour. Lean forward, look left. Still they trog past, mostly bunches of kids now, my age and a bit older. I pull back so they won't spot me.

Eleven o'clock. Bit quieter now I think, except somebody's shouting a few streets away. Sounds barmy: glad he's not shouting at *me*. I'm sitting with my knees drawn up and my arms wrapped round them, a position that has my bumbone in

61

hard contact with the floor. The sweater I'm sitting on feels about as thick as a cigarette paper. My jacket's zipped to the top and the collar's up, but I'm cold. I remember there's a pom-pom hat in my sweater drawer and tell myself it might as well be on Jupiter.

My knees hurt, and the base of my spine. I need to stand up or stretch out. It's still a bit early to try to sleep so I get up, and suddenly I'm desperate to pee. It's all that coke of course. It's only ten past eleven, I suppose I could find a kebab house or something, but I'm stuffed and I wouldn't have the cheek to go in and just use the toilet. I'd have to shove everything back in my bag too, and hope nobody pinched my doorway while I was gone. I decide to use the *en suite* facilities.

Across the street and down a bit there's a back alley. It's very narrow and inky black, and in normal circumstances I wouldn't go anywhere near it in the daytime let alone at night, but these aren't normal circumstances. Good thing is, it's so dark I won't need to go right in so I can keep an eye on my stuff. I cross over, dodge into the shadows and undo my jeans, and at that precise moment somebody turns into Barr Street.

I can't believe it. I've been sitting in that bloody doorway for an hour and a half and nobody's come past. Not a soul. Yet now, with my jeans down and my bum in the wind, suddenly this guy's coming towards me.

I tell myself he won't see me. It's so dark, if I stay absolutely still and hold my breath he'll pass the mouth of the alley without knowing anyone's here.

Doesn't happen like that. Just as I'm telling myself it's okay, he'll be past in a second, he turns into the alley. It doesn't *lead* anywhere. As far as I can see it just runs along the backs of some shops, it's where they keep their wheelie bins. It's only when he starts fiddling with his zip that I realize we've something in common.

That he thinks he's alone is obvious, but he'll certainly spot me when he turns to leave, and he might not be best pleased to have had an audience. It's an impossible situation. I've got about one second to reveal my presence before he starts hosing down the wall, but if I do he's going to catch me with my pants down and who knows what'll happen then?

It's now or never. I cough.

What . . .? He twists round, sees me squatting about a metre and a half away and goes, Oh I say, I'm most *awfully* sorry Miss. Seem to've blundered into the Ladies. *Do* excuse me.

I'm not kidding. He's zipped up and out of there before I can draw breath. I'm so relieved I relieve myself if you know what I mean, and by the time I'm decent and on my feet there's no sign of him. I have a little chuckle, crossing the street. I can't wait to tell Kirsty. She'll laugh her head off.

Nick

Sharp's Rents to Pulteney Court's a half-mile walk frou narrer, dirty streets wher ragged peeple walks or leans in doorways, their feets in black half-frozen slush. I leevs Ma and the little gels sleepin off that hyce-festival and trudges frou the dark to reech Pulteney Court befor seven. It's wery cold, but no chill strikes frou my stout boots, my greatcoat. Wen I gets there the door's shut but bootmarks in the new snow on evry step so Doctor Snow's here firs. I nocks, opens the door, peeps in. That lobby's dark, nor no sound neever, but lite up the far end. I shuts the door and clump clump clumps in them fine boots up the lobby. I'm neely there wen the doctor pops his head out. Good morning Nicholas, he sez. I see you are a paragon of punctuality.

I dunno wot is this *paragon of punchwallity* but mus be somfing good cos he's smilin. Yessir, I sez, bin won of them since I bin a nipper, and he larfs wiv his mitts in the pockets of his long white coat.

Firs work he givs me, sweepin. I'm to go outside, sweep all that snow off of the steps and clear a paff to the street. I done that wery quick cos I wants to keep my sitivation. What, done already, he sez wen I fetches the broom indoors, and he sticks his head out for a gander. Excellent, he sez, smilin. You shall have a title, laddie: Quick Nick.

How d'you like it?

Likes it wery well sir, I sez.

Splendid, he sez, then let it be Quick Nick.

He tels me keep my coat on, arst me do I know the coal-merchant Merriman.

Oh yessir, I sez, tho I never herd of him.

Take this note, he sez. I takes the note and he's watchin me. Can you read it Nick? he sez.

I looks at it and to tel the troof it aint up to much, this doctor's writing. I write same like this back in ragged school, Miz Lemnitz warm my arse wiv her switch. I don't *say* this o'course, just finks it. I can't read all of it sir, I sez, jus this middle bit wot it sez One Ton of best somfing-or-ovver Coal, and Pulteney Court witch I'm guessin at cos that's wher we are now.

Doctor Snow nods, smilin. Very good Nicholas, he sez, nor he don't call me *Quick Nick*, I spose cos my readin's slower'n my boots.

I arst free times wher is Merriman's yard and coms to it at last. *Doctor*, sez Merriman's cheeky clerk wen I hands him the note. *Doctor* Snow? Wot's a *doctor* doin practisin at Pulteney Court?

I sez, that's *his* bizniss, yors is coal. His mug turns red at that, he wants to swipe me upside the hed but a customer's a customer and a ton of coal's wot they calls a *hesteemd horder* so he daren't. I stares him down like a cove wiv a title and walks owt.

Nikki

Bit of luck, that unisex toilet affair. Guy might just as easily have turned nasty. I sit till one in the morning creating alternative scenarios. My eyes feel like they're burning while the rest of me freezes. I imagine one of those snowmen with bits of coal for eyes, only these coals are on fire.

I force myself to lie down with my feet inside the sweater. I can't lie on it *and* have my feet in it, so now the padding under me is even thinner. My hip-bone's pressed against the floor and it's a toss-up whether that'll stop me sleeping more than cold feet would, but there's no ideal solution and I've made my choice. I try to lie still so as not to kick the sweater off.

I've always been proud of my shape. People think I diet all the time but I don't. I'm one of those lucky people who can eat everything and not put weight on. I love the way I can see my bones in the mirror, but I'm getting the downside now and I wish I was like Janice at school. Allerdyce her last name's, but the kids have converted it to Lardarse and she'd be comfy on this floor. Comfier than me anyway.

I can hear a clock in the distance and I wish I couldn't. It chimes every quarter, and you wouldn't believe how long a quarter of an hour feels when you're sore and cold and scared. The reason I'm scared is, people walk past. I don't see them, I've got my eyes shut, but I hear their footsteps and I'm

66

like, what sort of people walk around London in the middle of the night? Crazy people, goes a little voice inside my head. Desperate people, people with nothing to lose. The sort of people who wouldn't think twice about sticking a knife in you to get sixty odd quid and a nice thick sweater.

It's a long, long time before I drop off. I do sleep eventually though, which is amazing. I *feel* as if I've been wide awake all night. I only know I've slept because of the dream.

I dream I've gone up to Yorkshire like Gran suggested. Walked all the way I think. Dad's place is this big old house by itself, trees all round. Wind is roaring in the trees, rocking their tops. I walk up this long gravel driveway and knock on the door. My knocking starts such a loud echo inside the house I feel embarrassed to have been the cause of it. I'm backing off ready to run when the door's opened by a woman wearing one of those short grey wigs you see lawyers wearing on telly. I go, Hi, I'm Nikki, I've come to see my dad. She says, you haven't encouraged him I suppose, swanning about the house half dressed? I say not *him*, I mean my *real* dad. Ah, she says, so you *admit* to having swanned, contrary to subsection seventeen of the voluntary code of conduct? No, I tell her, shouting. I haven't done anything, it's not my fault. Of *course* it's your fault. She sounds like a wasp. Family breakdown's *always* the girl's fault: goes back to the Garden of Eden, to Eve. She speaks to somebody I can't see. Take her down. She steps to one side and Ronnie darts out, leering, and that's when I wake up.

I'm so stiff you wouldn't believe. It's still dark but I can hear traffic, other noises, the odd voice. Oxford Street waking up. I don't know whether I'm glad or not. I'm relieved to have sur-vived the night but sleep hasn't refreshed me at all: I feel like a zombie. I stuff things in my bag, wondering if I can stand another night. And another. The only thing clear in my head is, I could murder a coffee.

Nick

D'you know what you are, Quick Nick? sez the doctor. It's seven o'clock and I bin shutterin the downstairs winder.

Paragon of punchwallity sir, I sez.

He nods. You're all of that and more, young fellow. Among other things you're a providential presence, a fortuitous find and a serendipitous servitor.

I hangs my head. I done my best sir, I mumbles, din't look to giv hoffence.

Offence. He larfs like a lion's roar. You've given no offence, Nick; precisely the opposite in fact. Here. He presses a shilling in my hand. Your day's wages, and now be off with you before your Ma fears you've frozen to death.

Anovver shilling and I keeps my place. I sings, walkin home in the hicy wind witch don't touch me no mor nor my fambly neever. The song I sings is won wot I composes inside my hed and it goes like this:

Quick Nick lucky Nick, happy wiv his station
Quick Nick lucky Nick, gorra sitivation.

Not wery good, but heard worse down the penny gaff and don't care anyway. I'm a servant in a doctor's house, witch it's not so good as a carpenter like Father but better'n pickin oakum in the workhouse, better'n a coal-merchant clerk.

I seen all over Doctor Snow's house today. It's got eight rooms, same like ours at Sharp's Rents but wivowt the forty-six peeple and one dog, and wivowt the stinkin cesspit under the cellar-floor. Won way me and that cheeky clerk the same tho: we boaf wondrin wot a doctor's doin in a thieves' kitchen like Pulteney Court. None of my bizniss I tels myself, but wonders abowt it jus the same. Wot sort of doctor's that Doctor Snow, I arst myself. The sort wot puts dosh in yor hand, I replies.

He don't sleep at Pulteney Court, witch is why I dint find no bedroom. I seen his doctor room downstairs tho. It's got work-benches same like Father's old shop but full wiv jars and bottles and such, bit like the pothacry. Nex to it I seen a room witch evry wall made of books, so Doctor Snow's a scholard alrite.

You fallen on yor feet Nick, I sez, witch it's wot Jack sez wen a cove wins at the tossin. Blows a sixpence on pies and hot tea I does, and swaggers home singin like a ruddy nightingale.

Nikki

I feel dirty. My jeans and jacket are crumpled and the skin round my eyes feels stiff because I haven't washed my face. I can't believe Mum used to have to *force* me to wash. Mucky little devils, kids.

It's five to seven. The big shops aren't open yet but I find one of those poky snack and sandwich places and go in, hoping I don't look too much like someone who'd slept in a doorway. I'm dying for the lavatory and there is one, but it'd be a dead give-away if I went straight to it so I get a latte and a Danish and sit down. It's lovely and warm in here. I want to put my head down and fall asleep but the only other customer, a thin guy in lycra with a cyclist's helmet under his chair is already giving me funny looks so that's nonstarter. I sip and nibble for a minute, then get up and carry my bag through to the toilet, hoping the proprietor won't think I've finished and clear or, what'd be worse, come after me and tell me to sod off.

Nobody follows me and I've got the place to myself. I use the lavatory then strip off my jacket, push my sleeves up and run water into the tiny basin. It comes hot after a bit and I plunge my hands in, luxuriating in the feel of it, bending over to splash my face and neck. A towel would've been useful at this point, so naturally I've neglected to pack one. There's one of those dispensers that lets you pull paper down and I use about a metre of it, dabbing myself half-dry. I'm rushing to finish before somebody else comes in. When I've damped and dragged a brush through my hair and I'm still by myself, I dodge back into the cubicle, lock myself in and change my knickers. I emerge with the used pair in my open bag intending to give them a quick rinse through, but my luck runs out. A grave-dodger comes in, shoves past me with a grunt and slams the cubicle door. I zip up the bag and return to my breakfast, which nobody's cleared.

The cyclist has gone. Two postmen have his table. They look at me, but only the way all men'll look at a girl by herself. I dunk my pastry to show I don't give a shit.

Leaving, on impulse I lean across the counter and murmur, you're not by any chance looking for an assistant?

I'm dead polite, not to mention being a customer, but the guy looks offended. Not by any chance darling, he growls.

Narky sod. I'm not using *your* bathroom again, I tell him, flouncing out.

It's nearly light on the street, starting to get busy. Four more shopping days to Christmas.

More wit and wisdom from Magistrate Stern: 1 December 1853

STERN: This is not the first time you've been up before me, is it?

DEFENDANT: No sir.

STERN: In fact, you have appeared in this court no fewer than eight times in the last two years, is that not so?

DEFENDANT: If you say so sir.

STERN: I *do* say so, you bold ruffian, and I confess myself astonished. Why, since you are invariably apprehended and punished, do you persist in committing these piddling offences? I've fined you, imprisoned you, even flogged you, and what is your response? Why, to break yet *another* baker's window and help yourself to his bread. Are you *mad*?

DEFENDANT: No sir: hungry.

STERN: We all of us grow hungry, fellow. *I* grow hungry. Doesn't drive *me* to sally forth armed with a large pebble and destroy a window pane belonging to somebody else. Why does it have that extraordinary effect on *you*, eh?

DEFENDANT: Begging your pardon sir but you has work, a hincome. I can't get work, sir.

STERN: Oh, and why's that, d'you suppose?

DEFENDANT: 'Cause I bin to prison, sir. Coves don't like to take a man on who's bin to prison.

STERN: Stuff and nonsense, man. I put it to you that you haven't *tried* to find work, that you've never been overly fond of it, that in fact you expend all of your energy and cunning in *avoiding* work.

DEFENDANT: 'T ain't *true* sir. I've tramped the streets *pleading* for work, *begging* for it, *any* sort of work. I've even offered to work for no wages sir, just wittles and a place to lay my head.

STERN: *Have* you now? Well, it so happens that I may be able to help you there. What d'you say to that?

DEFENDANT: I'd be greatly obliged sir.

STERN: So I should hope, fellow. Yes, I know of an enterprise which employs men on precisely the terms you mentioned a moment ago. It's called Millbank Prison, and you will go there for six months. Take him down.

Nick

Here Jimmy, I sez, bit more meat in this. He's knelt by the cold hearth same like always, fryin saveloys wot aint there.

He looks at the pie I fetch him. Can't fit *that* in my belly young fella, he sez, on top of all these sossidges.

Scoff the pie, I tels him, them sossidges'll eat cold tomorrer. I don't larf wen I sez this: only the mad larfs at madness.

He nods his shaggy white head. All rite boy, he sez. Thankee.

Fire on the hearth in our room, pan of real saveloys. My hart warms to see Ma and the little gels lookin fat in them new old cloves. Ma looks at me. Was the doctor satisfied wiv yor work, Nick? Will he need you tomorrer?

I told you Ma, I sez, I'm in Doctor Snow's household. He calld me lots of names wot I can't say: paragon of punchwallity one of 'em, serridippy-somfing and provvi-somfing else, but I finks he likes me. I'm to go evry day 'cept Sundays for a shilling a day.

We scoffs pies and tea like four toffs, 'cept toffs don't sit on puddly floors. Them saveloys too much grub so Ma tels Connie take 'em to Missus Plowman and her little wons acrost the passidge. Little Fan sucks mash-up pie and tea off of a spoon, witch it looks horrible but she don't look, jus paints her face wiv it. After, Ma sez, won't it be good if we could move from Sharp's Rents, go back to som 'spectable parish.

Yes Ma, I sez, but best wait eh, jus til we shor Doctor Snow meens to keep me on. We warm, I sez. Feets dry, Connie aint holdin horses' heds no mor. Father look down, he'll be happy I fink. Happyer'n befor anyway.

Evrywon so happy I sings my song for 'em. Connie larfs rite frou but that don't bovver me. Ma claps and sez, bravo Nick, let's have it agen, so I sings it agen and agen til some cove bangs on his wall, yells for me to stop my racket, witch it's cheeky cos noffing *but* racket at Sharp's Rents, wot wiv drunken men and squeekin rats and starvin babbies, but I stops cos we mebbe flit soon and that cheeky banger gotta stay, so we mor luckyer'n him.

Snow ficker and ficker on that rotten roof and colder'n the grave, but us Webley toffs sleeps the nite frou, snug as a bug in a rug.

Nikki

Feeling better for my wash and brush-up, my spot of breakfast, I hoof it up to Oxford Circus in plenty of time to beat the morning rush-hour. At the station I buy one of those three-day tickets tourists use: you can tube or bus all day long for three days, anywhere in central London. I figure if I'm looking for work and a place to stay I need to be mobile, cover as much ground as possible while daylight lasts. For starters I ride the Bakerloo line down to the Embankment. It's cold by the river but I know some places, eating places where I might get work.

It's a clear morning, and although the sun hasn't hauled itself above the roofs its watery rays are glinting off the top cars of the Eye, which is not revolving. First time I've seen it still. There's a coffee place in the old County Hall building, corner closest to the wheel. It isn't open yet, but it gets dead busy when the visitors start queueing for the ride. Now there's a van parked in front with its back doors open. Two guys're hurrying backwards and forwards, carrying flat trays of bread and stuff into the building. I lean by the plinth of Dali's soft watch with my hands in my pockets, waiting for them to finish. As soon as the driver starts swinging the doors shut I go across.

'Scuse me? I'm talking to the other one, a guy of about nineteen who looks Greek.

He eyes me up and down, scowling. Yeah?

Hi. I'm looking for work.

So?

Well, I was wondering if . . . I glance towards the building. He snorts.

You're a kid, we don't use kids.

I'm sixteen, I've waited on, cleared tables.

The driver laughs. If you're sixteen darling, I'm Robbie bleedin' Williams. What's up: arsed off with school I s'pose?

No, and anyway I wasn't talking to you.

Hooo! He grins at the Greek. Better watch her Georgie, she's one of them assertive women. *Will* be I mean, when she grows up. He swings himself into his cab, slams the door. The Greek looks at me, mouths something I don't catch because of the motor.

Pardon?

The van pulls away in a gout of blue pollution. I said get lost, he snarls. I'm busy.

How about asking the manager?

I *am* the manager. Go away.

I stick my tongue out at him which I suppose proves I'm underage, but still.

I walk on. It gets busier. I try every place I see, both sides of the river. National Theatre, Tate Mod, even the Globe, plus about twenty little places I don't know the names of. I offer to clear, to wash up, to take out garbage, to sweep. No dice.

My feet kill. I sit on a flat wall that freezes my bum. For something to do I switch my phone on and find Kirsty's texted: MamaNosYrsAf WAN2TLK?

Mum knows I'm safe which is good, and of *course* I want to talk unless she means Mum. I want to talk to *Kirsty*. I send back: THNQTLK2U1230

Roll on.

Letter to the *Sunday Telegraph*

Sir

Your correspondent E Gatley (2/12/02) asks why, when our politicians have promised to be tough on crime, is crime on the increase? I would have thought the answer was obvious: tough on crime is just not tough enough. A century and a half of pleading and whining by so-called prison reformers has taken away from the authorities every punishment the criminal class once feared: punishments such as the treadwheel, the cat o'nine tails and the rope.

The nineteenth century thug didn't get counselling, he got a damn good hiding and he didn't come back for another. The lazy lout was put to hard labour, which I have no doubt did him a power of good. And if a man committed murder he didn't spend a few years in a centrally-heated cell writing his memoirs before being released to kill again: he was strung up in front of the public he'd offended and that was the end of him.

It's high time we took a fresh look at the old, tried-and-tested methods, instead of bending over backwards to understand. It's the criminal who needs to understand, and there's no teacher like pain.

Your sincerely
Cleasby Nossiter

Nick

Nex mornin I'm sweepin doctor's lobby wen he coms owt of his workshop wiv a fat glass jar in his hand. Nick, he sez, I want you to take this jar along to the Bridle Street pump and fill it with water.

I looks at him. *Bridle* Street sir, I sez. I'm serprised cos Pulteney Court has its own pump not ten steps from the door.

The doctor nods. I want water from the Bridle Street pump, Nick, and nowhere else.

Wery good sir, I sez, and I takes the jar and I walks frou the slush down Great Pulteney Street, along Silver Street and up Bridle Street to the pump.

Ther's a hidle loafer leant agin the wall at the corner of Great Pulteney Street and Silver Street, I seen him watch me go by. He's stil ther wen I coms back wiv the jarful of water and he larfs. Looks hevvy, he sez. Wot's rong wiv Pulteney Court pump, or Broad Street com to that. Both nearer'n Bridle Street.

I looks at him. I'm my master's servant, I sez. My master wants water from Bridle Street, I fetches it from Bridle Street. He want snow from the Norf Pole I'll wade frou all this snow to fetch it, tho it be zacly the same as wot I'm wadin frou.

He larfs again. Won't catch *me* slavin for no barmy toff, he sez.

No, I sez, that's why I'm in a sitivation and yor proppin up a wall.

He dint know how to anser wen I sez that.

Wen I fetches the jar to Doctor Snow he smiles. I expect you're wondering what sort of establishment you've become a part of eh, Quick Nick?

No sir, I sez, witch it's a lie.

Oh come now. There's a perfectly good pump in the yard, yet your master sends you through ice and snow to fetch water from another pump some distance away and you don't wonder why? You disappoint me, Nick.

I looks at him. I got curiosty sir, but Ma sez it killt the cat.

He larfs. Your Ma's right young man, but the saying ought to go that *idle* curiosity killed the cat. Idle curiosity's a vice, whereas active curiosity's what distinguishes us from the animals.

I don't unnerstan so I keeps mum and he sez, do you know what cholera is, Nick?

Course I do, I sez, it's the plague, and he sez, that's close enough but d'you know what *causes* it?

Me sir, I sez. I'm a carpenter's son, don't know wot cause noffing, 'cept sawdust.

He larfs. I don't know either Nick, but that's the conundrum that exercises *my* curiosity, and I've a feeling water comes into it somewhere, in fact I *know* it does. He smiles. All I have to do now is prove it, and that's the business of the establishment you have joined.

I dint know it sir, I sez, finkin if I *did* have knowd, mebbe I wouldn't be here. The mad larfs at madness, but *nobody* larfs at cholera.

Nikki

I ride up to Piccadilly Circus. There's loads of little caffs in the narrow streets of Soho. Maybe my luck'll change. Coming out of the station I look at my watch. Twenty past twelve. I walk over to Dunkin' Donuts, buy my lunch, get a corner seat and fish out my phone.

Hi Kirsty it's me.

Knew it would be. How you doing, where are you?

I'm good and I'm in Dunkin' Donuts.

Which one?

Never mind. What happened with my mum?

Don't ask.

Why, was it bad?

You could say so. She wouldn't believe we only talked once. Says if you didn't call me I could always call you. I told her I keep trying but your phone's never on. She says what about *text*? I goes, I've left five messages, no reply. I don't believe you, she says, so I'm like, look Mrs Minton, she asked me to tell you she's safe and I've done it. I can't do any more. *You* try phoning her.

What did she say to that?

Said she had, hundreds of times but your phone was off. Yes well, I says, it's the same with me.

Then what?

Nothing. I broke it off.

She didn't say anything when you told her what I said: you know, about it being true about Ronnie?

Not really, no. She went quiet for a bit, then said she didn't believe any of it.

Oh well. Thanks for calling her anyway.

You thanked me already.

I know but . . .

What about last night, did you get a room, where'd you sleep?

I slept in a doorway.

God, you must've been *frozen*. Haven't you any dosh left? Surely you could've got a room for one night.

What'd be the *point*, Kirsty. I have to start skippering sometime, might as well get used to it.

I suppose so, but . . . I don't half wish you'd picked a better time to leave home, Nikki. I mean, Christmas in five days, I don't know if I can stand the thought of you out there in the cold while everyone else is . . .

Not *everyone*, Kirsty. I'm not the only one out here, you know. And I didn't pick the time, Ronnie did. Or maybe the time picked me. Anyway I don't want you worrying, spoiling your Christmas. Just have your phone on at half-twelve and I'll be fine. Hey, you'll never guess what.

What?

I think I met the weirdest guy in London last night.

Go on.

So I tell her all about Mister Zippy. She laughs like I knew she would. I think you better make yourself a big luminous LADIES sign, she says. Prop it up when you need to water the pavement. Then she says, hey listen Niks, are you sure he was

84

actually *there*? You're not, like, *hallucinating*? You know, with cold or hunger or something?

I'm not *hungry*, you div. I've got a really scrummy hot choco- late fudge doughnut steaming in front of me right now. And you don't hallucinate with cold. You just drift off to sleep and never wake up.

Oh *shit* don't say that, Nicks. I'll lie awake all night tonight now, thinking about you.

Well don't, 'cause I won't lie awake thinking about *you*. Listen, this doughnut's staring at me, begging to be eaten. Same time tomorrow, eh?

Y . . . yeah, I'll be here. You take care now. I love you.

Love you too Kirst. Bye.

It's getting hard, pushing that *no* button.

Nick

I walks into Sharp's Rents and sees two boys in Jimmy o'Dowd's room, no Jimmy. Oy, I sez, wot's yor little game eh. Look at me wery bold they does and won of 'em sez, wot bizniss is it of yors. The big won sez it, nor he aint wery big at that.

This is Mister o'Dowd's room, I tels him, and Mister o'Dowd's a wery good frend of mine.

He larfs. Then you got a good frend up Bedlam, mister.

Bedlam, I sez, wot's this you tellin me?

Cove wot livd here was took, he sez, nor I aint lookin to see him back neever. Mister Sharp giv me and him a penny to make the place reddy for a fambly.

They got a broom, a pail and a shovel so I got to bleev 'em. I don't say noffing else to 'em, carry the bread and tea I brung to our room. Wot's this abowt Jimmy, I sez.

Ma shakes her hed. Jimmy bin eatin rats, she sez. A wisitin reverend catches him at it, tels Mister Morgan, and Mister Morgan sends for Doctor Lankester.

That Mister Morgan 'spector of nuisances, Doctor Lankester hofficer of health.

Lankester takes won look at poor Jimmy, sez Ma, rat twitchin in his teefs, blood runnin down his chin, orders him carted away to the madhouse. She seen a tear on my cheek and sez, Jimmy be warm at Bedlam, Nick. He'll have wittles and a bed, witch it's mor'n he had here.

They beats 'em in the madhouse Ma, I sez. Chains 'em to the wall and beats 'em, nor nobody never seen 'em agen neever. Old Jimmy better *ded*, Ma.

Praps Jimmy don't fink so Nick, she sez. Mebbe he'll be happy. Who knows wot'll make a madman happy?

Not whips Ma, I sez. Not fetters. Oh I *wish* he hadn't of went. Look. I brung him bread.

Ma looks at me. Mebbe he's got better'n that son, up Bedlam. She smiles, takes my hand. Let it be Nick, she sez. You done yor best. Noffing we can do now. Take that wet coat off and have som food. Yor sisters've bin waitin.

I drinks my tea but can't eat noffing. Ther's a little cove inside my head wisprin, over and over, *nice bit 'o rat that, nice bit 'o rat that, nice bit'o rat.*

Nikki

So, nothing doing on the Embankment. I ride back to Piccadilly Circus with sore feet and Kirsty's words echoing round in my skull. *Christmas in five days, I don't know if I can stand the thought . . .*

I'm not sure I can stand it myself. I left home with the idea of finding somewhere to live and a job, not dossing in doorways. The chance of getting something seems remote now. Probably there was none from the start.

Christmas is special to me. Not the religious aspect, though the sound of a choir singing Silent Night always makes me want to cry. It's more the way it seems to make all sorts of people *kind*, even if it is only for a few days. They go *Merry Christmas* to complete strangers, geezers they'd look straight through the rest of the year. Just yesterday I saw this guy, guy in the City by the look of him, holding the door open for two women coming out of Selfridges laden with parcels and smiling while he did it. Any other time he'd probably have let it swing shut in their faces and laughed as he strode away. It reminded me of old Scrooge in the film, going out of his way to be nice to everybody after the spirits have finished with him.

What I'm saying is it's *people*, the way it changes them for a while that makes Christmas special for me, and this Christmas I won't be with people. I'll wake up alone in some doorway and for the first time in my life, Santa won't have been. I won't watch our Marie practically diving into her pillowcase, pulling out parcels, tearing off strips of red and green to see what she's got. No appetizing aroma will drift through from the kitchen and there'll be no radio softly playing carols. All this goes through my head as the train sways and roars the two stops to Piccadilly and – I'm not kidding – I very nearly give in and go home. It's only imagining Ronnie, tiptoing into my room at midnight with a bulging pillowcase and another bulge which is his special present to me that keeps me from doing it.

I don't know it yet, but something's about to happen under the statue of Eros that'll change my Christmas prospects a little bit for the better, and my longer term prospects very much for the worse.

Lot to answer for, old Eros.

Nick

Can't help it, I'm frettin abowt madness and the cholera. Got to tork to sombody. Nex day I'm luggin some boxes from the lobby, stackin 'em in a corner of the workroom. Doctor Snow's at the bench doin fings wiv his jars of water. I'm passin him and I sez, beg pardon Doctor, and he looks round.

What is it Nick? he sez.

I bin finkin sir, I tels him.

It can be a rewarding occupation, Quick Nick. He smiles. What have you been thinking about?

Wot you tolt me yestday sir, I sez. I bin finkin, have I gone and took a sitivation in a plague house, mebbe carry the cholera to Ma, the little gels?

He shakes his head. This is no plague house Nick. It's a laboratory. I give you my word that you are as safe here as anywhere in London. Do you believe me?

Course I bleevs you sir, and I fanks you for settin my mind at rest. Sir . . . ?

Was there something else, Nick?

Yessir. Would a cove know if he was goin mad, sir.

The doctor sets down the jar he bin workin wiv, stares at me. This cove, he sez, would he be yourself, Nick?

I looks down and wispers, yessir.

And you think you're losing your mind?

Yessir.

And what makes you think that, Nick?

So I tels him as how I seen King Henry's table in the middle of the road, all set owt for a banquet.

Tell me Nick, he sez wen I'm done, when you saw this sumptious feast, how long had it been since your last substantial meal?

Substa *wot*, sir, I sez.

He smiles. How long since you'd enjoyed a really good blowout?

I has to fink. 'Bowt a week sir, I sez. Longer mebbe.

He nods. Do you know what the word *hallucination* means, Nick?

I shakes my head. Sounds like free words sir, nor I don't know any of 'em.

He larfs. Well Nick, sometimes our eyes play tricks on us. We seem to see things which aren't actually there. We call these *hallucinations*, and one of the conditions which can give rise to them is starvation. You're not going mad Nick: you were starving.

These doctor words eases my mind but makes me fink of Jimmy o'Dowd. I tels him abowt Jimmy and his save-loys wot aint ther and he sez, there you are, you see: the starving often hallucinate food.

But sir, I sez, they carts Jimmy off to Bedlam yestiday for bein mad. Mebbe he aint mad, jus starvin.

He nods. Possibly Nick, though since I did not see let alone *examine* Mr o'Dowd, I really cannot say. He smiles a sad smile. There's many a lunatic in Bedlam as sane as you or I Nick. We know no more about insanity than we do about cholera.

Dangerous gel, I finks, that *Lucy Nation*.

Nikki

It's really nippy but there's people sitting on the steps under the statue. Three Japanese draped in expensive camera equipment. A hippie couple. A bag lady. I can't decide between Dunkin' Donuts and McDonald's. I drift across, put my bag on the step and sit down, wondering how long it takes for cold stone to give you piles.

I don't know what to do. I'm depressed as hell at the thought of sleeping rough again, but going home's a nonstarter. What I'd *like* to do is go south of the river, down to Balaclava Road, ask Steve Patten if I can change my mind. It's *so* tempting but I mustn't. Mustn't, because I know that if I did I'd never want to leave and that wouldn't be fair on Steve. This is my problem, in spite of what he believes. *Mine*.

Hi. A girl looking down at me, hands in the pockets of her black jeans. Fifteen or sixteen. Spiky blonde hair, violet eyelids, pockety leather jacket, Nikes. I nod.

Hi.

You sound down.

I *am*.

I seen you from over there, looking lost. How old're you?

Why? It's nice she came over and all that, but I don't think I should tell her all my business.

She shrugs. Just wondered. Run off, have you? She's looking at my bag.

93

I nod. Yeah.

Don't talk much, do you?

I don't know you. What d'you want?

Don't want *nothing*, just being friendly. Where you staying?

Nowhere. Anywhere. I stand up, lift my bag. She puts a hand on my sleeve.

You don't have to go, I won't eat you. On the street you mean?

Yes, just till . . .

That's what we all say, *just till*. Listen, I know somewhere.

What, a hostel or something? I'm not . . .

No not a hostel, a house.

A squat?

Yeah but like, it's warm and dry. Well – she grins – *dry* anyway.

And you're inviting me, are you. Why?

Oh, 'cause I'm one of them whatchamacallit, *procurers*, that's it. I *procure* young girls for this sinister Arab-type guy who packs 'em off to the Gulf to be these like, *hostesses*. It's part of the white slave trade.

I've irritated her, she's winding me up. I shake my head. Look, I've got to go, so . . .

Got to *go*? Urgent appointment with a doorway I suppose. Go on then. See if I care. She turns, starts to walk off.

Wait . . . I don't *mean* to call after her, I do it without thinking.

She turns. Look, *I* haven't got all day either so make your mind up.

I have. I'll come. Thanks.

And that's how it starts. My life of crime I mean.

Nick

So evry day I sweeps, carries, runs herrands: shilling a day, shilling a day til by and by com Christmas Eve and I'm doin the shutters and Doctor Snow come owt on the step and rubs his hands togevver and sez, I'll not be needing you tomorrow Nick. No Christian gentleman works on Christmas Day.

Is that *jus* tomorrer sir, I sez. I'm not to be let go, I hopes.

The doctor shakes his head. Let go Nick: *you*? Why, I don't know how I ever managed without you. In fact, if you'll have the goodness to stay a few moments longer you shall have a small token of my esteem.

Doctor Snow's got a cartful of wery long words and I don't always foller wot he sez. Anyway he goes off, coms back wiv a big fat parcel wot I fink mebbe got all them words inside.

For you and your family Nick, he sez. Merry Christmas.

Hevvy, that parcel. Hevvyer'n babby Fan.

Fank you sir, I sez, oh fank you, and he sez, it's nothing Nick. A few trifles to mark the festive season.

So I lugs this parcel frou the hyce and snow to Sharp's Rents, to my warm fat fambly and we opens it up and this is wot we finds:

Won plump capon.

Won plum puddin.

Bottle of gin.

Bag of filberts.

Bag of tea.

Four rosy happles.

Free pair of fick mitts for Ma and the gels.

Two wool mufflers for Connie and Ma, won wool blanket for Fan.

Won little purse wiv a sovrin inside. A *sovrin*.

Oh *my*, how we makes merry nex day! Merriest Christmas Sharp's Rents ever seen I'm sure. For dinner ther's capon and plum puddin and peas and potatoes, all cookt at the baker's down the road, and to foller we has froot and nuts and tea and a bowl of smokin bishop. We got so much grub, Ma sends Connie acrost to Missus Plowman wiv dinner for her and the nippers, and this sets us finkin abowt Mister Plowman at Millbank and Father in heaven and Jimmy o'Dowd up Bedlam and all the ovver poor souls, so it aint *all* merriment, nor it dint ought to be neever.

He sees us Ma, I sez. Father sees us, full and warm and happy.

And she sez, know what Bedlam meens Nick?

I shakes my hed.

Bethlehem, she sez.

Nikki

I follow her underground, watch her feed the ticket machine. Two to Paddington. She scoops out the tickets, heads for the platform with me trotting at her heels going, what do I owe you, you don't have to . . .

She shakes her head. Don't matter, sort it later.

Okay, but tell me your name. I'm following you and I don't even know what they call you.

Demi.

Really. Demi as in Moore?

Yeah.

What's it short for, Demi?

Don't ask *me*.

But it's your name, surely you must know . . .

She shakes her head. I didn't say it was my name, it's what they *call* me. What's yours?

Nikki.

And that's your *real* name, yeah?

Course.

Yeah well, a lot of us don't use our real names 'cause there might be people looking for us and we might not want to be found.

Oh. We're standing on the platform. It's pretty busy. I imagine looking round and seeing Ronnie coming towards me. I shiver and say, I don't want to be found, d'you think I should give myself a nickname?

She shrugs. Up to you.

I think for a minute, shake my head. No, think I'll stick to Nikki. There's thousands of Nikkis, more than there is Demis anyway.

A train pulls in. We board, sit down quick. A lot have to stand. The doors close and we're off. I wonder what I'm doing letting this girl, this Demi, take me I don't know where. What if . . . I look at her. What you said before, you know, about being a procurer. You weren't . . . I mean, you were joking, right?

Oh for Gawd's sake. She looks at me, half amused. You're thirteen, aren't you?

No.

Fourteen then, tops. Yes, I was joking, Nikki. She chuckles, shakes her head. Good job I found you, you wouldn't last a week on your own.

I'm stung. I did all right last night, I retort, and the night before. I've all I need in here. Kicking my bag. And I've got dosh too.

Sssh! She glances round. Why don't you just hang a sign on your back: *I'm loaded, mug me*. You might as well.

I feel my cheeks go red, stare at my bag, feeling a div. The train stops, starts again. I don't look at her, don't say anything. She thinks she's my flipping *mother*, I tell myself. Think I'll get off, find myself a nice deep doorway.

I don't though, because the words *nice* and *doorway* don't belong together, and because having this streetwise girl beside me makes me feel sort of looked after. She's not my mother, but my mother's not available and yes, I *am* only fourteen.

Nick

D'you know what this is, Nick? Doctor Snow don't jus have me fetch and carry; he teech me fings as well. It's the day after Christmas and I'm rinsin owt jars in the workroom. I bin for water and its wery cold, slippy hyce all round the pump and my hands freezin. I sets the pail down and looks wot he got on the bench and I seen a silvery puddle like the hyce owtside.

I fetch a cloff sir, I sez, but he larfs and sez, watch, so I watches. The doctor pokes that puddle wiv a glass rod looks like a hycicle, and it com all to little silver balls wot rolls abowt. I shakes my head. No sir, I sez, I dunno wot it is. Somfing wet like water. It's not wet, he sez, and it isn't water. It's mercury.

Mercry, I sez. Must be a licker sir, same like gin. Gin com into my hed cos my hed hurtin wiv yestday's gin.

Doctor Snow larfs. Mercury isn't a liquor Nick, he sez, it's a metal.

Garn, I sez, before I can stop myself. *Garn* aint somfing you sez to a toff but the doctor only larfs.

It's true, Nick, he sez. Mercury's a metal.

I bleevs you sir, I sez, but it looks like you can't make nails wiv it nor pails neever, so wot's it for.

Oh, he sez, it has its uses Nick. It's a medicine, a poison, an essential component of thermometers, and the hatter's

99

trade would be sunk without it. *I* intend using it to extract the oxygen from specimens of night air.

I don't unnerstan *oxijen* nor most of the words he raps round it, so I nods like a scholard and sez, ahh. The doctor looks at me like he's waitin for me to arst him somfing so I sez, wot you want to hextrac that oxijen for sir, and he coms owt wiv abowt forty fousand big words witch I dunno how they all can fit inside one man's hed. *Cholera*'s won of 'em, and *miasma* and *analysis* and I dunno wot all. I stands ther noddin and ummin, wisht I never arst. All at once the doctor bursts owt larfin and sez, oh Nick, there's a scholar inside you and I intend to release him little by little.

I don't unnerstan that *scholard inside me*: I never et no scholard. I picks up the pail and goes back to rinsin, witch it don't take a cartful of big words to do. Doctor Snow's watchin me acrost the room, smilin in his eyes.

Nikki

It's five minutes from here she says as we leave the station. She sets a cracking pace, me practically trotting to keep up.

You still haven't told me why you want me at this squat, I pant. She doesn't say anything, just grins.

I hope you're not . . . you know, leading me into an ambush or something. Mates waiting to roll me for my dosh.

She snorts. I asked you before you mentioned any dosh, remember?

Okay yeah, but I still don't get it.

You will. This is it: home sweet home.

It's a dilapidated three storey with boarded-up windows in one of those rundown rows that used to be posh but are mostly bedsits now. Chained to the area railings is a beat-up bike with its front wheel missing. Dusty steps lead up to a cracked and blistered door whose transom has the only unprotected glass. Demi's knuckles rap out a code: two, four, three. A slice of face appears in a gap between boards at the ground floor window. Seconds later somebody draws a couple of heavy-sounding bolts and the door opens a crack. The same slice of face appears and a husky voice goes, who's she?

Name's Nikki, says Demi. Stop pissing about.

The crack widens. Demi turns. Come on Nikki, shift your arse. I'm still in two minds but I can't stand dithering forever. I join her on the top step and she shoves me through the gap. I'm standing on cracked tiles in a musty hallway. When she follows me in and slice-face slams the door it's practically dark.

Nikki she says, meet Tan. Slice-face sticks out a paw. Pleased to meet you Nikki, how d'you get involved with *this* degenerate?

Hi Tan. I er . . . we met in Piccadilly Circus.

Nikki's dead naive, says Demi. A babe in the wood. I came to her rescue, didn't I Nikki?

Well . . .

That's a yes, she says. Come and say hello to the others.

My eyes are adjusting to the gloom. I see the missing wheel propped against a wall and a flight of stairs going up, before Demi drapes an arm round my shoulder and steers me through a doorway that has no door.

We're in the front room. What light there is has two sources: the gap in the window boards and a fire in the hearth on which bits of the missing door are crackling.

There are three guys in the room, one kneeling in front of the fire and two inspecting me from a saggy old sofa. One of these looks at Demi. Better odds now then, eh gel: two against four?

Demi nods, grinning. Better believe it, Arrow. Guys, this is Nikki. She turns to me. Nikki, the dysfunctional beside Arrow is called Monkey, and the scally by the fire's River. These are the misfits I've coped with alone, like Snow White and her dwarfs. She smiles at me. Now you know why I brought you here. I need an ally.

Don't you believe it, goes the guy by the fire. He stands up, wipes his hands down the sides of his jeans. He's about six-two, very thin with a bumpy shaved head. She's a dictator, old Demi. Rules us with a rod of iron. Ain't that right, lads?

Nods from the others, murmurs of assent. Tan says, we're

hoping you'll be a whatsit on her: mellowing influence. Think you can sort it, do you?

He's got a nice face now I can see it all. Rest of him's nothing special though: around five-five, Elton John figure stuffed into four old jackets. I shrug, look at the sticky carpet and mumble, Dunno. I'll do my best.

Arrow laughs, shakes his shaggy head. Mission impossible, kid. *Nothing* mellows our Demi, not even Leb Red at twenty-five the eighth. Never mind though, eh. At least you'll have a roof, bit of grub now and then. Better'n out there.

He's got that last bit right. I mean okay, I feel like I'm naked, all their eyes on me, but at least I'm not *scared* of them. There's something makes them nonthreatening, their sense of humour maybe. I'm not letting my guard down mind, not yet, but I feel fairly safe. I can imagine sleeping in this house and believe me, that matters.

Nick

Wen I done wiv the jars, Doctor Snow arst me wot I knows abowt air. Never finks abowt it sir, I sez, cos it's same like finkin abowt noffing.

Nothing, Nick? he sez.

Well, I sez, you can't see it nor hear it nor taste it nor feel it: jus breeve it. Air's jus anovver word for noffing if you arst me.

He larfs and sez, air's a mixture of gases, Nick. They're invisible, like your poor friend's saveloys, but unlike the saveloys they exist. We can't see them but we're surrounded by them, we move through them every moment, without them we'd die at once. The main ones are oxygen, nitrogen, hydrogen and carbon dioxide.

I looks at him, wafts my hand abowt. Don't feel like my hand's hittin *won* fing sir, never mind four.

More than four, he sez, because all sorts of things are carried on the air: particles.

Sounds like *hycicles* sir, I sez.

He smiles. These particles are minute, Nick, too small to see except through a microscope. There's pollen, soot and dust – some dust is sloughed-off human skin. There are millions of these particles. We breathe them in and out. Some doctors say that's how cholera comes to us, and plague, and other diseases; that they are borne on the night air, or on foul-smelling air. It's called *miasma* theory, it's utter nonsense, and I'm working with specimens of air to try to disprove it once and for all.

I looks at him. Why sir. Why you doin all this wiv the air and the water and that.

He smiles. Mankind needs a cure for cholera Nick, and we cannot know where to begin looking for a cure until we know what *causes* it. To proceed without that knowledge is to be a man looking for a collar-stud in the sands of the desert while wearing a blindfold.

Wen the doctor sez this I gets a picter in my hed of a blind cove crawlin over hot sand, feelin all abowt for that collar-stud, and I wisht I got words in *my* cart wot'll make picters same like that.

I tels him and he smiles. You shall have them Quick Nick, he sez, in the fullness of time.

After, moppin the lobby I sez to myself over and over, *in the fullness of time*, finkin, som words better'n ovvers. Can't see 'em nor touch 'em, but I can taste 'em in my mouf and feel 'em round my head and I'll have 'em all, *in the fullness of time*.

Nikki

Great Scott, what *must* you think of me? The one called Monkey jumps up from the sofa, motions for me to take his seat. He doesn't *look* like an old-fashioned gentleman, and hoots from the others confirm he's being satirical but I play along, dropping a mock curtsey, going why *thank* you, kind sir and sitting down in what I hope is a demure manner, my knees pressed together.

Great Scott, splutters Arrow. He's laughing so much the sofa's shaking. Where does he *get* 'em from, the donkey?

Old films, says River. Forties costume dramas, he's mad on 'em. Aren't you Monkey, you sad bastard?

Monkey looks disdainful, shakes his head. I don't need films to show me how to behave, you ruffian. You forget I'm the younger son of an Earl.

You're the younger son of a *bitch*, goes Demi. How come you never offer your seat to *me* then?

One offers one's place to a *lady*, he tells her. Scrubbers don't count. Beneath one's notice, scrubbers are.

Beneath one's *blanket* you mean. This from Tan. Everybody cracks out laughing, even me, but the blanket bit starts me wondering about the sleeping arrangements here.

Turns out there's nothing to worry about. Tan goes off and comes back with six cracked mugs of coffee, and when we've drunk them Demi rescues me from Arrow's question about why

I left home by offering to show me round. We visit a kitchenful of used crockery and another downstairs room which is cold and bare and half-wrecked, then climb the stairs to a landing with three doors. Demi opens the first. Bath and toilet, she says. I glance in, nod. It's pitch dark and pongs a bit. She doesn't open the next door, just nods at it. Lads sleep in there, this one's mine. She smiles. *Ours* I should say, if you decide to stay I mean. She opens the door and we go in. It's the front bedroom. The window's boarded up but one panel has been removed. It's getting dark outside but a streetlamp throws a square of light on the floor. The room seems full of beds: in fact there are four, all singles. Only one's made up. Demi nods at it. Mine. You get to choose from the rest and don't worry: there's blankets in the bottom of the wardrobe, pillows too. Not a snorer, are you?

I shake my head. Not as far as I know. You?

She chuckles. I haven't had any complaints.

I look at her. You've shared before, then? Here I mean.

Oh yes. People come and go, same as any squat.

Who'd you share with last?

She pulls a face, says, why?

I shrug. Just wondered. Don't tell me if you'd rather not.

I'm not bothered. Sandra, she called herself. Might have been her real name.

How long ago?

Dunno. Couple of months maybe.

Why'd she leave?

Demi snorts. The usual: she got into a relationship with one of the lads and one of the others got heavy about it. You know, jealous. There was a big row and she walked out. Lad went with her: Doggy-bag he was called, don't ask me why. Better without 'em anyhow. She looks at me. Best not to get involved, Nikki, romantically I mean. Always ends in tears.

I nod. I don't want involvement, Demi; refugee from it in fact. I just want to be left alone.

She smiles. Good, well you'll be fine with the rabble downstairs. They may look like they've escaped from somewhere but they're all right really. Have been with me, anyway.

I smile back. I'm glad. It *feels* okay, you know, like a home?

She laughs. I wouldn't go *that* far, kiddo, but at least you know you haven't been abducted. Come on. Let's sort you out some bedding.

Nick

Wen the little gels sleepin I tels Ma wot Doctor Snow teld me. Wot I *'members* of it. Mercry, and air wot aint won fing but four, and fousand fousand little stuff floatin abowt wot you needs a mikerscope to see – soot and pollen and that. He's lookin for wot brings cholera, I tels her.

Why? she sez, same like I arst the doctor.

Cos he's got to know wot bring it befor he can find a cure.

Fancy, she sez.

O yes, I sez, to proceed wivowt that nollidge is to be a man lookin for a collar-stud in the sands of the desert wile wearin a blynfol.

She looks at me serprise. You torkin *toff* Nick, she sez. No call to *tork* toff jus cos you sweeps for won.

I shall tork toff, read toff, *write* toff, I tels her, in the fullness of time.

Ma's mouf drops open like a gaspin cod. Fullness of time, she sez. Goodness, yor Doctor Snow must be a better teacher'n Miz Lemnitz.

Yes, I sez, and he don't take no switch to my arse neever.

We larfin fit to wake the little wons. After a bit Ma stops larfin, grabs my arm. Oh Nick, she sez, see ther, how water's pourin thro the roof, we'll all be flooded out.

I looks and it *is* pourin. Floor mosly puddle already and we dint notice, we was larfin that hard. Quick Ma, I sez, take little Fan, I'll wake Connie. Them little gels still half-sleepin as we bundles 'em along the passidge to the street door, pushin and shovin wiv evryone else. Owtside, the court fills up wiv forty-five peeple and won dog, cos all the rooms is flooded same like ours. So much push and shove, shoutin and screechin, no one finks wot *causes* this flood til I yells *look Ma, snow's meltin!* Minnit I sez this *evryone* notices, and they starts to dance and skylark.

Forty-five peeple and won dog com to ninety-four bare foots, and every won of them capers and kicks and spins on the snow til the snow com slush and the slush com water and evryone black wiv mud and singin fit to burst.

Nikki

Demi helps me make up my bed, then we go downstairs. Tan and Arrow are on the sofa; there's no sign of the other two. I sit down on a wooden chair sort of looking round for them but I don't ask. None of my business. Arrow must sense I'm wondering though because he says, Monkey and River out on business, Nikki. Evening shift.

I nod. Oh.

You hungry? goes Tan.

I'm not sure if he's asking everybody or just me. I look at Demi, sitting cross-legged on another chair. She smiles. There's no regular mealtimes Nikki, we eat when we get hungry. You want a sandwich or something?

Well I . . . is anyone else having anything?

Doesn't matter says Tan, getting up. It's no big problem, a sandwich. You eat meat?

Y . . . yeah, I eat everything. Oh, except mushrooms. Can't stand mushrooms.

Well good 'cause we don't have any. Corned beef okay?

Lovely.

He grins, crossing the room. Can't promise lovely but it'll fill up a hole.

Thanks. I watch him go out, trying not to think about the kitchen I glimpsed. When he's gone I look at Demi. What happens about money here?

She laughs. Same as anywhere else, it goes out faster'n it comes in.

No I mean like . . . corned beef's not cheap and he's putting it in a sandwich for me. I should give something, you know, towards it.

Arrow chuckles. It's a slice of tinned meat kid, I wouldn't worry about it.

I shake my head. I'm not worrying Arrow, but I'm not free-loading either. I've got . . . a few pounds, in my bag upstairs. I'll just . . .

In the morning, goes Demi as I start to get up. You can make a contribution in the morning if you insist. In the meantime try to relax, okay? We wouldn't be offering grub if you weren't welcome to it.

Being in an unfamiliar house and meeting all these people, I haven't noticed how hungry I am. When Tan brings my sand-wich I attack it like a wolf. He's brought a glass of milk too, and I drain it without taking the tumbler from my lips. I don't even feel embarrassed till I've finished and Tan growls, I wouldn't've bothered getting that if I'd known you were only going to pick at it.

Arrow nods, laughing. Pick, as in pick and shovel you mean?

That's the one.

I feel myself go scarlet from the neck up. I . . . I'm sorry, I didn't . . . I don't usually . . .

Take no notice kid, says Demi. Wait till you see *these* two tossers eat, it's like the pigs in *Hannibal*.

That's a dirty lie! protests Arrow. Me and Tan can polish off a dead villain loads quicker than them, *and* we keep our sty clean.

Ooh, I don't know about *that*. She looks at me. You saw the kitchen, didn't you? Well it's *their* job to keep it tidy.

I nod and smile but I don't say anything. I'm too new to risk criticizing the housekeeping. Might take a stab at it myself tomorrow, if they'll let me.

Nick

Now here's a funny fing. You waits for somfing bad to pass, and wen it's gone you finds ther was somfing good abowt it. 'Cept the toothache o'course: *noffing* good about that.

Take the cold. Wen I walks owt of Sharp's Rents nex mornin it's mild. *Mild*'s a scholard word and I likes it. It's good the hyce is gone, but everyfing's black and brown and gray agen. That hyce and snow coverd all over evryfing see, made it look white cleen like a toff's mouf, full of shiny teefs. *Mild* makes London smile, show her rotten teefs.

Oh, and the stinks is back. London got lots of little rivers: little Fans and Connies wot runs into the big won, the Thames. Evrybody's slops get frowd in them little rivers, dogs and cats as well, even babbies somtimes. Stinks somfing fearful them rivers, speshly in hot wevver but here's the fing: all the time they bin froze up, no stink at all. Now the *mild* unfreezd 'em and it seems like they bin savin all that stink inside the hyce in case we bin missin it.

Wen I walks up Pulteney Court, firs fing I spies is Doctor Snow on the step. Blessed relief eh, Nick? he sez wiv a sweep of his arm. Work for your mother and sister again soon, I shouldn't wonder.

Yes sir, I sez, and plenty foul air to look for them particles. He larfs and I looks at him. You'll not be turnin me off sir, I hopes, now the freezin's gone?

He shakes his head, lays an arm acrost my sholder as we goes indoors. I've told you before Nick, I don't know how I ever managed without you. Speaking of which, we've got a frightful mess upstairs I'm afraid, which I'm relying on you to clean up. He smiles a sad smile. Leaky roof.

I looks at him. Leaky roofs is wot my father mended sir, I sez. I could take a look if you'd let me.

He frowns. I'm not sure about that, Nick. Those old tiles're bound to be slippery. Suppose you fell: what would become of your family then, eh?

I'd take care sir, honest. I means to foller Father, but not that way.

Well. He looks at me in the dim lobby. Mop up the water and I'll think about it. And in the meantime I must sally forth with my faithful pump and try to capture a measure of that foul air you mentioned just now. He smiles. D'you think you can take care of the premises till I return, Quick Nick?

Yessir, I sez. Evryfing be took care of, you'll see.

Who's this *Sally Forf*? Pal of *Lucy Nation* mebbe, but not my bizniss so I gets my mop and pail and goes upstairs.

Nikki

Feels funny going to bed with a stranger in the room. Demi's lent me a nightie, which is good because that's something else I didn't think to pack. I get ready in the bathroom. There's no bolt, but Demi says nobody'll burst in without knocking. There's no electricity in the house by the way. It's been turned off, but they've got a boxful of those little lamps that'll freestand or stick to walls. They're battery-powered and light up when you touch them. Once it's dark everybody carries one when they leave the front room. In the light from my little lamp I can see that the bathroom is as grotty as the kitchen. Long time since Mr Ajax popped his head round *this* door.

Demi seems to be asleep when I return to the bedroom. I drape my clothes over a chairback, get into bed and lie listening to the wind. It's a wild night, bitterly cold, and I'm glad I'm not in some doorway. Not that it's particularly warm in the room. The meagre heat from the fire downstairs doesn't reach here, but there's plenty of bedding and I'm soon feeling cosy, a luxurious sensation deliciously enhanced by the booming of the wind outside I feel secure too, which is weird in a houseful of strangers.

I sleep.

I wake early, but lie till Demi stirs.

Morning.

Uhh . . . morning Nikki. Forgot I wasn't by myself. Time is it?

I peer at my watch. Quarter to eight.

Ugh! Feels like the middle of the night.

It's the dark.

I know. I hate this time of year. You want the bathroom first?

What about the guys?

Hoo, you're joking. They won't stir for hours yet.

Can I get a shower?

Demi snorts. *I* wouldn't. Local pool's got showers, we go there once or twice a week.

That's cool Demi. I'd never have thought of that.

You learn to use what there is. Go on. I'll have another five minutes. Ten, if you're gonna get squeaky-clean.

Loud snores from the guys' room as I pass. I strip-wash in icy water and get my kit on fast. I rinse a few bits through as well, though the sliver of soap won't lather. Someone's fastened a piece of string above the grotty bath. I drape my washing over it, though it'll take days to dry. I brush my hair in the spattered mirror, carry my little lamp back to the room.

Demi groans, shields her eyes. That wasn't five minutes.

No, it was thirteen, I washed some things.

Too pure to live, you are. Why don't you go down the kitchen, put the kettle on, make two coffees? I'll be down in a bit.

What *is* there? To boil the kettle I mean?

Oh, it's a camper stove: canned gas. You'll find a lighter somewhere. Oh, and don't fill the kettle right up, Nikki. We haven't cracked lifting those canisters yet and they cost an arm and a leg.

I don't get that last bit, that's how naive I am. It's days before I suss I've fallen among thieves.

Diary of Solomon Stern, Magistrate:
17 January 1854

Dined with Pashley at my club. He told me an extraordinary story about some young fellow calling himself a doctor, who's set himself up in premises at Pulteney Court and claims to be seeking the cause of cholera. *The cause of cholera*, if you please. It seems to me that some people have been beguiled into believing that, because we British can cross land and sea with unnatural speed using the power of steam, because we have learned how to span wide rivers with mighty bridges of iron, because we are carrying God's word into the uttermost parts of the earth, we can do *anything*. Such overweaning pride is highly dangerous. It is bound to lead to a great and richly deserved fall.

I blame the Great Exhibition.

Who *is* this puffed-up medico? Who does he *think* he is? What sort of a doctor would choose a rookery like Pulteney Court from which to conduct his practice? I'd pay a guinea for a glance at the fellow's diploma.

The cause of cholera! Might as well seek the cause of storms, or lunacy, or crime. *Sin* is the cause of cholera, Doctor. Human wickedness.

Everybody knows that.

Nick

Doctor Snow don't use upstairs but he knows this: let a puddle lie upstairs, that puddle com downstairs quick and not by way of the stairs neever. Ther's a brown stain on the seelin in the room wiv all them boots and cloves, anovver on the floor under it, so it's happend befor. All I has to do wen I gets up ther is find the room wot's over the cloves room and ther's my puddle. It's not wery big, I mops it up easy, then goes lookin for the trap wot leads to the roofspace.

Turns owt the trap's in the seelin of the landin. It's way above my head so I goes scoutin for a ladder. Don't have to scout far: ther's won in a corner of the cloves room. I clects a candle as well and some loosifers and takes 'em all upstairs. I sets up the ladder and climes to the trap. Under me's a longish drop to the lobby floor. *Never look down*, Father use to say and I don't, not after that won time.

Trapdor lifts away nice an easy. I sticks my head and sholders frou. Pitchy dark, 'cept won little glim wot shows me wher is the hole in the tiles. I lites my candle an goes up, takin care to stand on the joists so I won't fall frou a seelin. I moves carefully tord the glim, wisprin *in the fullness of time* over and over, witch it aint somfing Father use to say.

Mus be my lucky day cos I finds the fault is won wot

I can mend easy wivowt climin to the roof. Over agin the kingpost, one tile has slipt the lead hook it's spose to hang to. It's still ther, witch is lucky cos mosly a slipt tile'll slide down the roof and be lost. Lucky too the wind aint got frou the hole, blowd mor tiles off. I holds up the candle to hinspec the dammidge. The batten is wet wot holds the hook, probly rotten, two rafters wet as well. Father on this job, put in new timbers but I can't. I sticks my fingers frou the hole, gets a hold on a corner of the tile and starts workin it back up, hopin it don't slip away down the roof. It's takin a wile, nor it aint done wen I hears Doctor Snow callin me.

I daren't let go the tile. He calls and calls, voice comin closer til he's under the ladder. Nick, he shouts, you're not on the roof I hope?

No sir, I sez. Doin the job from underneaf.

Good man, he sez, so he aint finkin of dismissin me, witch it's a releef.

Tile's reddy to go back on its hook. I slides it in, workin the top edge under the tile above, bottom edge over the tile below, witch it aint easy. Wen it's back in place I bends the soft lead wiv my fumbs til the hook grips tite. Wen I tries to wiggle the tile abowt it don't budge. *A good job well done*, Father use to say.

Wen I coms down, Doctor Snow arsts to know all abowt it so I tels him. 'Twere jus a tile slipt its hook sir, I sez.

Hook? he arst.

Yessir. Tiles hangs to lead hooks on battens. This one'd slipt sideways, that's all.

And these battens Nick, he sez, what do *they* hang to?

They doesn't hang sir, they's nailed acrost the rafters.

I see. And each tile has its own hook, is that right?

Yessir.

Well, I've learned something today Nick, thanks to you. He smiles. *And* we have a sound roof, also thanks to you. Your father would be proud.

I'm proud. 'Taint *evryday* a coster's boy'll mend a roof an teech a doctor. I'll be ridin in a bleat'n carridge nex.

Nikki

You managed the stove then? Demi joins me on the sofa, reaches for her coffee.

Yeah, no prob. You off out this morning?

Course, living to earn you know.

I'm surprised but try not to show it. I'd assumed she was unemployed. What d'you do?

I'm in retailing. Fashion.

Bet that's interesting. *Dressed like that*?

It has its moments.

Are you in one of the big stores?

Sometimes, but I do boutiques too: stock control.

Oh. I don't suppose . . .?

What?

You couldn't put in a word for me, could you? I really need a job.

She pulls a face. I could ask I suppose. Trouble is Nikki, you're underage and look it. They're gonna wonder why you're not in school.

I could make myself look older, change my hair or something.

Yeah, well . . . leave it with me okay? I promise I'll think about it.

Thanks Demi. Can I do you some breakfast?

She shakes her head, drains her mug, stands. No time. Catch you later, yeah?

When she's gone I sip my coffee, wondering what to do with my day. I've more or less decided I'll stick around for a while, provided nobody objects. My alternatives are pretty poor anyway, at least till I get a job. The sixty-odd pounds I've got won't last long but it might let me pay my corner till I start earning.

It's half-nine. No sign of movement upstairs. I've turned the gas right down under the kettle and spooned coffee powder into four mugs. I put a drop more water in the kettle so it won't boil dry, wondering if I dare carry drinks up to the guys. I decide I'd better not, without really knowing why. Instead I start searching cupboards and shelves for cleaning materials. The place badly needs sorting, especially this kitchen and that bathroom, so maybe I can make myself useful in that way until I find a job.

There isn't much. Whoever shops evidently doesn't have domestic hygiene as a priority. When I've plundered every cupboard and fought my way through heaps of trash in a truly disgusting pantry, my total haul amounts to a zinc mop-bucket, a handle without a mop, some stiff grey cloths and a mildewed cardboard drum half-full of damp scouring powder. There isn't even any washing-up liquid.

I go to the foot of the stairs and listen. Nobody's stirring, so I give up on keeping water hot for coffee, fill the kettle and turn up the gas. At least if I get a bowlful of hot water I can start making inroads on the stacks of dirty crockery which cover every flat surface in the kitchen. And if the gas runs out: tough.

Nick

So the days goes by and it com Febry. I'm sweepin, carryin, runnin errands, evry day 'cept Sundays. Doctor Snow's started loanin me books for Sundays; wants I should himprove my readin. You'll not be sorry Nick, he sez. It will stand you in good stead someday. I bleevs him, but it frightens me havin them books at home. 'Spensive, books is, an ther's coves at Sharp's Rents wot'll nick 'em soon as spit.

Cold coms back, tho not so cold like befor. Work coms Ma's way, little bits of stitchin for a milliner. Connie helps her wiv it. Two of us ernin wages, Ma starts savin pennies in a can wot she hides under a hearthstone. Now we got books and dosh to fret abowt, witch it's a worrit but better'n starvin.

Fings lookin up wiv us. Won day I walks by Jack's cart, firs time since he giv me them four happles. Hallo Jack I sez, I owes you for fruit.

He looks at me. Nick, he sez, I seen you comin along, dint reckernize you. Fort it were som toff lost his way. You growd *fat* my son, prosprous. Where's the gold-mine? He's herd som scholard reed from the paper, how fousand coves findin gold in Australia, comin milliners overnite.

No goldmine Jack, I sez, an I tels him all wot happens

to me, Doctor Snow and evryfing and he sez, my *hat* Nick, but you've fallen on yor feet and no mistake.

He won't take my money tho. Them happles was a gift, he sez, a gift to a friend. He smiles a sad smile. You could start back nipperin for me Nick, but I spose it don't compare to hobnobbin wiv doctors and dukes and hearls and such.

I larfs. Aint seen no dukes yet Jack, nor hearls neever; aint bin *hintrodooced*. Spec I will be mind, in the fullness of time.

Eh? He looks at me, shakes his head. I finks you better make yourself scarce Guv, he sez. This aint no place for a scholard.

We're still mates tho, Jack and me. The Sunday after, he fetches his donkey and cart and moves me and Ma and the nippers wiv all our worldy goods out of Sharp's Rents to a house Ma's took in Pollard Lane. *Hole* house. No dukes lives in Pollard Lane, but no thieves lives ther neever, an no unforchnate women. Doctor Snow's books be safe here, and Ma's pennies. We be safe *ourselfs*.

One little bit of bizniss waitin tho. I've forgot it but it aint forgot me.

Nikki

Bloody hell! I turn, up to my elbows in scummy water. Tan's leaning on the doorframe in jeans and singlet, a shirt draped over his shoulder. He nods at the stack of gleaming plates on the drainer. You're fond of a treat aren't you, tackling that lot?

I shrug. I was up, thought I might as well be doing something. Kettle's on for coffee.

Oh cheers. He lifts the kettle, upends it over a mug. Having one yourself?

No thanks, I had mine with Demi.

She gone, then?

Yeah, while back.

He milks his coffee from a carton. The milk's past its sell-by: it cracks as it hits the hot drink, speckling the surface with white flecks. Bugger! goes Tan, I *hate* that.

I nod. Me too. I'll get some fresh when I shop this morning.

Shop?

Yes. We need washing-up liquid, a mop, disinfectant.

He smiles. You should've asked Demi, she'd've got it for you.

No need, I've got dosh. Anyway I want the stuff this morning so I can spend the day fixing this place up a bit.

That bad, huh? he grins.

Oh, I didn't mean . . . I suppose I'm being cheeky, I hope you don't mind.

Course not Nikki, far from it. We *need* taking in hand, sorting out a bit. We tend to let things slide, see?

Arrow sticks his shaggy head round the door. Morning Cinders, hope you've not forgotten to polish my shoes, give my coat a brush. Oh and by the way, I like my bacon crisp.

For a second I'm not sure if he's serious: I open my mouth and nothing comes out. Tan rescues me. Bog off Arrow, you scruffy git, he says. You wouldn't recognize a polished shoe if it jumped up and kicked you in the mouth. He grins at me. Take no notice of him darling, he's a brain-dead tunnel dwarf with smelly feet and holes in his underwear. Brought up in care, you know.

I'm not sure how I'm supposed to respond to this, so I smile and go back to my dishes. Arrow makes himself a coffee and both lads leave the kitchen. A radio comes on in the front room. It doesn't look as though Monkey and River are getting up just yet, so I empty the kettle into my washing-up water and carry on till there's no more room on the drainer. There are no tea towels, so I'm stuck till I've been down the shops. I look at my watch and it's just after nine. Robbie Williams is belting something out on the radio. I leave the kitchen and go upstairs for my bag and jacket.

Nick

I trust yesterday's move went well, Nick? It's Monday mornin, I'm givin the doctor's bookshelfs the once-over wiv a fevver mop.

Oh yessir, I sez, fank you for arstin. Went off perfic.

Splendid.

That's the word alrite: splendid. Evryfing splendid wiv me today. Ma and the little gels too, o'course. Hole house close to our bread, my place wiv Doctor Snow, Ma's milliner work. Plenty warm cloves, good wittles evryday. Larfin, that's wot we is. An to fink a few weeks back we was in the shadder of the workhouse. *In the shadder of the workhouse* is somfing Doctor Snow sez the ovver day wen he's torkin about peeple wot's fallen on hard times. Who knows, he sez, who among us might not be driven to crime, were we to find ourselves living day in, day out in the shadow of the workhouse. I shivers wen he sez that. I can fair feel that shadder clingin like a damp sheet, like a shroud to my skin. Man can make a cove feel like that wiv his words, find wot cause cholera easy.

Speekin of witch, I'm runnin them fevvers along a line of books wen a title catch my eye. My reedin comin on a treat now the doctor teechin me, an I reeds this on the spine of a fin, fin book: *THE MODE OF COMMUNICATION OF CHOLERA*. Course I can't reed *all* of it, just reckernize the last word, *cholera*, and Doctor Snow's name after. Sir, I sez, book here got yor name on it.

Yes Nick, he sez. That's the paper in which I set out my argument for contaminated water's being responsible for the spread of cholera. He smyles. I might have saved myself the trouble though, since nobody paid it the slightest attention. Some prefer the old bad air theory, and others cling to the even older notion that epidemics are sent by God to punish us for our sins. The lazy man's explanation I call that: sickness, crime and anything else you care to mention, all attributable to the evil in men's souls. He smyles again. It's cheap, because we needn't spend money in research, and it spares us the bother of thinking. The only trouble with it is that things get no better.

I don't know noffing about God and 'tributable an all that. Dunno wot the doctor's talkin abowt reely so I does wot I always does: ums and arrs and nods, hopin I sounds like a professer wot's too busy to anser, too busy wiv his fevver mop.

An then the bell rings an I goes to anser the door wiv the mop in my hand an finds two coves on the step: a Peeler, an the bake potato man.

Nikki

Arrow points me towards the local shops, a row of six under a tower block a couple of streets away. One's a minimarket, which is what I need. The others are a hairdresser, a betting shop, a pizza takeaway, a chemist and a newsagent. They've all trimmed their windows except the betting shop.

There aren't many people about: two mothers with buggies and three guys doing something down a hole. The hole reminds me of Kirsty because last year at this time we were passing one every morning near school. We never saw anyone working on it; it appeared two weeks before Christmas and when it was still there in the New Year, Kirsty christened it *the hole of the Christmas period*. Roll on half-twelve, I'll remind her of her joke.

Me and the two mothers have the minimarket to ourselves. I get the milk first in case I forget, then start loading cleaning stuff. I get washing-up liquid, wire-wool scouring pads, a bottle each of pine disinfectant and bleach, a pack of dishcloths and two tea-towels. They don't have heads for mops, so I splash out on a new one. I get a broom as well, and a scrubbing-brush and a brush and dustpan set. It comes to seventeen eighty-eight, so I hope Demi and the guys don't decide to boot me out any time soon.

The stuff's heavy and awkward and I'm sweating when I get back.

Arrow's on the step. You found it then?

Yeah.

Nice one. He relieves me of the mop and broom, props them in the hallway. Must've cost you a packet, all this. We'd have got it for you, you know.

Yes I know, but I wanted it first thing. Anyway it makes me feel better, making some sort of contribution.

I know what you mean. It's just, dosh don't last forever, y'know? Even when you've got a stash, and there's cheaper ways of getting stuff like this. That's all I'm saying.

I can't think of a suitable reply, so I don't say anything. He helps me lug the stuff through to the kitchen. I nod at the camper stove. Is there a spare canister for that?

He shakes his head. I can bring one this aft, though.

Yes, please. I just hope it lasts till then. I'm going to be using a lot of hot water.

Get a fire going in the front room. It won't give you *hot* water, but it'll warm it. Those canisters're hard to come by.

I know, Demi told me. How much are they? I'll give you the dosh.

Save your dosh. I told you, I'll fetch one.

What do I burn on the fire?

There's the remains of the back room door, and we've started on the skirting in there too. I'll rip some out and get it started before I go, okay?

Yes, thanks. I'll carry on in here then.

Arrow goes off. I'm drying plates and stuff, and I can hear him and Tan pulling the house to bits. It reminds me of an old movie I saw once on telly: a paddle steamer's crossing the Atlantic and they run out of coal, so they start tearing up all the wooden parts of the ship to feed the furnace. It's like the ship's *eating* itself, and it makes you wonder how much of itself it can consume without sinking.

I just hope the house doesn't fall on me while I'm cleaning it.

Nick

That's him, sez the bake potato man, the minnit I opens the door. *That*'s the cove wot pincht my potater.

I dint pinch noff . . . I starts to defen myself, then breaks off cos I 'members.

Wot's up sparrer, sez the Peeler, cat got yor tongue?

It . . . it was weeks ago hofficer, I sez, and 'twere only won little potato at that.

Oh, so you don't deny pinchin it then, that won little potato?

No hofficer, I took it all right, but I were starvin an it were rollin on the ground.

It were rollin, sez the bake potato man, cos you stirred up Patch and he upset the can.

I dint stir him up, I com for a warm and he goes for me.

Oos this Patch? sez the Peeler.

Dog, sez the bake potato man.

Oh, sez the Peeler.

My head's in a wurl, can't bleev all this wot's happening. Fings bin goin so *well*, that lark wiv the potato cleen gone from my mind, and now . . .

The Peeler's torkin, lookin at me. So a potato wot's rollin belongs to him wot can catch it, is that wot you finks?

No, I . . . I *dint* fink, I was hungry.

I fink you better com alonga me, young shaver. Magistrate'll know wot's to be done wiv you.

Bot'ny Bay, sez the bake potato man, *that's* the spot for him. He'll not be needin a warm from nobody's potater-can there.

What is it Nick? Doctor Snow coms owt, seen the Peeler. Is anything the matter, officer?

The Peeler knows a toff wen he hears won. Ho yes sir, he sez, this gentleman as made a hallegation against the boy, and the boy's confest.

Confessed? sez Doctor Snow. Confessed to *what*?

To pinchin a harticle of my property sir, sez the bake potato man, to wit, won ot potater.

The doctor looks at me. Is this true Nick? Did you steal this fellow's potato?

Yessir, I sez.

But *why* lad? Don't I pay you enough? He looks . . . *dispointed*, witch it makes me feel bad.

This was *befor* sir, I sez, the wery day you firs seen me on this ere step in fac. I wouldn't do noffing like it now sir, indeed I wouldn't.

Doctor Snow looks at the Peeler. You heard the lad, officer. He was hungry when I found him; in fact he was starving. He's part of my household these days, and a different man entirely. I believe I can promise you, that nothing remotely like this . . . er, hot potato incident will ever occur again, and if this gentleman – he looks at the bake potato man – will be so good as to inform me as to the value of the stolen item I will reimburse him at once, in cash, so that we can put this unfortunate and somewhat *trivial* business behind us.

Oh no sir, sez the bake potato man, jus wen I'm startin to feel releevd. No no, that won't do at all. You see sir – he looks up at the doctor – ther's far too much of this thievin goin on, an it falls to us huprite citizens to see as the thief wot gets took is properly punisht, ovverwise wher's it goin to stop? No sir, I'm resolved to press charges, as is my rite, and to see this young ruffian transported or sent to prison.

Transported? scoffs Doctor Snow. For one poxy potato?

'Tweren't poxy sir, 'twere a prime potato, sez the bake potato man. Hofficer, do yor duty.

Well, befor I knows wot's wot the Peeler's got me in chancery an he's pullin me down the steps.

Courage Nick, calls Doctor Snow from the doorway. It's a misunderstanding, it will all be sorted out.

I *wants* to bleev him, but somfing tells me it won't com owt easy as that.

Nikki

'Lo Kirsty, guess who.

Not Helena Bonham-Carter *again*?

'Fraid so.

Where'd you sleep last night Niks? I couldn't stop thinking about you.

Well you can stop fretting Kirst, that's the good news.

What d'you mean: what's the *bad* news?

I'm with some people Kirst, in a house. Bad news is, it's a total tip. I've spent all morning scrubbing it and I still wouldn't rent it to a pig.

She laughs. Who are they, these people? Are you sure they're all right?

How d'you mean *all right*? None of 'em's Fred West if that's what you mean. None of 'em's Ronnie, come to that. There's a girl, calls herself Demi, and four guys who go by nicknames too.

Four *guys*? You want to watch it Niks. Sounds like a Snow White situation to me.

Naaa. None of 'em's a dwarf, Kirst.

Even worse if they're big, innit?

Turkey. How're *you*, anyway?

I'm good, except everyone's sweating those last-minute preparations, you know how it is.

Yeah, I know, Christmas. Hey Kirst, remember last year, that hole on the way to school. *The hole of the Christmas period*?

Oh yeah. Fancy you remembering that. Never thought *my best friend'll do a runner a year from now*, though.

No well, I didn't know myself. Anyway, there's one for *this* Christmas too. A hole I mean. Clocked it this morning by the shops.

What shops're these, Niks?

My turn to chuckle. Never give up, do you Kirst?

You're my friend Niks. I miss you, want to give you your present.

You got me a present?

Course, always do.

I know but . . . it's different now, isn't it? I haven't got *you* one.

Well of *course* you haven't, silly. I don't expect one. You need your dosh. Are you – you and the dwarfs I mean – are you doing anything for Christmas?

I dunno Kirst. We're not trimmed up or anything. I don't know how people in squats celebrate Christmas. There's no festive grub about but some of the guys're out at the moment so who knows, maybe they'll bring something back. We cook on a camper-stove though, so a fifty-pound turkey's not really an option. Listen, can I ask you to hang on to my present till it's safe for us to meet up?

Course Niks, as long as it takes. Listen, you take care, all right? I'm glad you've found a place but watch your back, and don't go trusting people too much. 'Specially them dwarfs.

I laugh. I'll watch 'em Kirst, don't you worry. I'm planning a stew for when they get back from the mine. Talk to you tomorrow?

You better.

That magistrate again

STERN: So without the slightest provocation, you goad the fellow's dog into upsetting his potato-can and send hot potatoes rolling in every direction.

NICK: Sir, I never provoked the dog. I just hoped to get a bit of a warm from the can. The dog went for me, sir.

STERN: The dog went for you, did it? I suggest the opposite is true: that you went for the dog. You're nothing but a common dog-stealer, are you? You saw a fine terrier and you thought to yourself: here's a fine terrier; I know a man gets up rat-matches who'll pay a guinea for a dog like this one.

NICK: No sir, I don't know nobody what gets up rat-matches and I've never stole a dog. My father was Daniel Webley, the carpenter.

STERN: This court wouldn't care a fig if your father was Lemuel Gulliver the pisser-out of fires. *You* sir are a potato-thief, a dog-stealer and a liar under oath.

NICK: 'Taint true sir.

STERN: So *I'm* the liar, is that what you're saying?

MAGISTRATE'S CLERK: Sir, there's a gentleman in court, asks to be heard on the subject of the defendant's character.

STERN: His *character*. I think the court has formed a pretty clear picture of the sort of character it is dealing with, but very well, let him step up, administer the oath.

SNOW: The defendant Nicholas Webley is well known to me, I employ him at my laboratory. For some weeks now he has . . .

STERN: Just a minute sir, aren't you the medico the whole city's tittle-tattling about? The one with rooms at Pulteney Court, claims to be seeking the cause of cholera?

SNOW: The same sir, though I hadn't realized I had become the subject of gossip. As I was saying . . .

STERN: And have you discovered the cause, Doctor?

SNOW: I believe so sir. Contaminated water is almost certainly the cause.

STERN: Indeed? And crime now, I suppose you know what causes *that* too, hmm?

SNOW: I'd hazard an educated guess, though it's not my field.

STERN: Pray enlighten us, Doctor. What is your *educated* guess?

SNOW: Hunger, squalor, despair: in short sir, poverty.

STERN: Balderdash! A pox on all your guesses, Doctor Snow. Sin, *that*'s the cause of cholera, *and* crime, *and* all the other miseries we're beset by. And the cure, sir, is what I like to call the three Ps: prayer, punishment and penitence. So your quest is a waste of time, you see.

SNOW: Sir, my purpose in coming here today . . .

STERN: . . . is *another* waste of time.

SNOW: I think not. Nicholas Webley comes of a respectable family, fallen on hard times through the premature death of his father, a skilled tradesman. Since that tragic event, in spite of his youth and the rigours of a particularly severe winter, the boy has succeeded through hard work in supporting his mother and two infant sisters, preventing them from becoming a charge on the parish. His theft of a single hot potato was a momentary aberration, occasioned by near-starvation, and I feel confident that this court . . .

STERN: You feel confident sir, because you think you know better than almighty God. The saintly portrait you paint of the defendant is a gross distortion: Webley is in fact a cynical young villain, apprehended while standing on the very brink of a life of crime. He will go to prison for one month.

NICK: But sir, my mother . . .

STERN: Your mother produced a thief, she must suffer the consequences. Take him down.

Nikki

Zounds, what sorcery is this? Monkey, just out of bed, stands gob-smacked in the kitchen doorway. I stop dicing carrots long enough to give him a smile. Like it?

Like it? I feel like the old woman whose vinegar-bottle got turned into a palace.

I pull a face. Hardly a palace, but thanks. Water's hot for coffee.

So *that*'s what's meant by instant. He pours, stirs, grins. You're a genie Nikki: the genie of the lamp. He hears footfalls on the stairs and calls, hey River, get a squint at this.

River pokes his bald head round the door. Blimey! I *thought* I heard somebody banging about earlier. What'd you *do* Nikki, wet the bed?

Course not, what d'you *mean*?

Monkey chuckles. You'll have to excuse my undereducated friend sweetheart. It's his crude way of asking what got you up so early.

Oh. I shrug. Wasn't early, River. Demi and the others had left.

Right. River's smile has an apology in it. Seemed early to me 'cause I sleep half the day. And like he says, I'm under-educated so take no notice. This coffee for me?

They take their mugs through to the front room and the radio comes on again. I look at my watch and it's five past two. I finish the carrots, add them to the spuds and onions in the big pan. None of this stuff was here of course, it took a second trip to the minimarket and another six quid out of my stash. I got a tin of steak and a pack of stock-cubes as well as the veg. Now I'm on pins in case the gas gives out, because I really want to give the dwarfs this stew, don't ask me why.

It happens at half-past three. I'm giving the stuff a stir when there's a popping sound and I look under the pan in time to see the pinky-blue flames die. Drat! I throw the wooden spoon at the sink, spattering the tile surround I've just cleaned.

Monkey, who must've been passing, looks in. Lawks-a-mussy, what's ado?

Bloody *gas*, that's what, I snarl. I'm not in the mood for old movie dialogue.

Unfazed, he peers into the pan. Hmmm. What if we whip it through to the other room and stick it on the fire, Niks? I bet it'll cook just fine if we keep it well stoked-up.

We do, and it works, and the appetizing smell's only half the reason I'm dead chuffed. The other half's that he called me Niks, which is Kirsty's name for me. Silly I know, but it makes me feel accepted.

Nick

Ther's wot they calls a *noldin* cell under the courthouse, and that's wher I finds myself. Ther's a downtrod-lookin cove ther alreddy wot I finks I seen befor. He looks at me. Dint do you no good then, he sez, all that fetchin and carryin? Wen he sez this I rekernize the sculkin loafer wot larft at me fetchin water from Bridle Street.

'T aint none of my master's doin I lands up here, I sez. Stuck up for me in court, the doctor did.

The loafer larfs. *That*'d set the magistrate agin you for a start, he sez. Can't abide a scholard, old Stern. Wot d'you get?

Get?

Aye. How long?

Oh. A monf.

Ruddy *monf*? That aint no *sentence*, that's a long *weekend*. He starts larfin; I bet he'd slap his knees if his hands weren't manacled.

Wot're you, I sez, the larfin loafer? I *hates* the cove.

Ooo, he goes, oooha-haa-haaa: sounds like Jack's donkey. Good name, he sez, *the larfin loafer*. Better'n the won the Beadle gimme anyway.

Beadle?

You heard. *Swubble*, he decides to call me. I arst yer,

was ever a horfan saddled wiv a darfter moniker than that? Mind you – he larfs agen – *his* name weren't much better. Bumble, like some bleedin' *bee*. And he's off agen, larfin.

I can't larf. I sits on the cold floor wiv my back agin the wall, lookin at the manacles on my rists, finkin abowt Ma and the little gels. She won't know wher I am, Ma. Wen I don't com home she'll fink me run off or killt. I feels badder abowt that than prison. I can do the monf, if only Ma knows wot's becom of me.

The loafer, Swubble, gone quiet: used up all his larfs. I don't want to tork to him but has to arst him somfing. Swubble? I sez.

He looks at me. Wot?

Wen they sends a cove to prison, do they tel his fambly?

Wot . . .? Oh aye lad, he sez. Magistrate sends his own carridge wiv a *hurgent* messidge, and half-a-crown from the poor-box to sweeten it. He can't hardly get *sweeten it* out for larfin, the barset. I turns my hed away, won't let him see me cry.

Nikki

There y'go, Kid. Arrow, first back, upends the plastic carrier. Tins thud on the worn carpet, roll about. He grins. More gas than Adolf Eichmann.

Monkey's wince is exaggerated. I say, steady *on* old chap, our guest could be of the Hebrew persuasion.

I shake my head. I'm not.

She isn't a guest either, says River. Sniff up.

Arrow sniffs the air. Hmmm, good smell. Old canister lasted out then eh, Nikki?

I indicate the hearth. Not quite.

Ah, right.

Hooter's working okay, says River. What about your eyes?

Arrow looks round the room, shrugs.

Kitchen, pursues River, try 'em through there. Bathroom too, if you're going up.

When he's left the room I scoop up the canisters, put them back in the bag. Six, I murmur. Thought we were short of dosh?

Monkey smiles. Cheaper to buy in bulk, Niks.

River nods. 'Specially the way Arrow does it.

Somebody mention my name? Arrow comes in, smiles at me. Great job, Kid, unbelievable. Reminds me of when I used to stay at the Copthorn Tara.

Huh! Monkey's expression is sardonic. Didn't know the Tara took guys who've been barred from the Sally Army, Arrow.

While the three of them bat put-downs back and forth I kneel at the hearth, feeding the fire with splinters and stirring the stew. It's thickening nicely; we're only waiting for Tan and Demi. I've decided if neither of them brings anything Christmassy, I slip out tomorrow and get a few bits to surprise everybody with.

Demi gets back at six o'clock. She detects the aroma when she's still in the hallway. I hear her ask Monkey about it. It's that genie you found, he says. She's swapped our vinegar bottle for a palace and magicked a few kitchen scraps into a stew to die for.

Demi sticks her head round the door. Nice one, Nikki, down in a minute. She's got two bulging carriers which she takes upstairs. Tan arrives before she comes down.

The stew's a hit. Everybody has two helpings except me; I've been sipping and nibbling all afternoon. They're all really nice to me, about the meal and the cleaning. I nearly tell them I could do a lot better if there was a vacuum cleaner. What stops me is remembering the expressions on Monkey's and River's faces when they were explaining the six canisters.

Nick

It coms alrite abowt Ma cos Doctor Snow visits me in that noldin cell befor they carts us off to Millbank. Ther's nine of us in the cell by this time, mosly thiefs and wot they calls *unforchnate wimmin*, witch means wimmin wot sel therselfs. Oh Nick, sez the doctor wen the turnkey lets him in. I spec he's com to tel me I'm dismist wivowt a caracter, but he aint. Oh Nick, he sez, what an awful place. Looks like he mite cry. No help to me you mite fink, doctor standin ther lookin miserble but you be rong. I seen how upset he is and I finks, fank God it's *me* got a monf not the doctor, cos he'd *die* at Millbank.

Don't upset yorself sir, I sez, Nick aint scairt. Nick'll be splendid inside, get owt in the fullness of time.

He tries for a smile. You *are* splendid inside Nick, he sez, and your place will be waiting for you when you're released. I'm only sorry I failed you in that travesty of a magistrate's court.

I shakes my hed. It's of no consqense sir, I sez, and I'm ever so obliged you aint dismist me. Can I arst you to see Ma Knows Wher I am?

Swubble bin lisnin. Wen I sez this he larfs. Oh aye, he sez, be sure to tel his *ma* sir, so she mite fetch his warm bread-and-milk of an ev'nin, tuck him in for the nite.

I spec the doctor to hignor that loafer but he don't. He

don't. Wot he done is, he grabs his dirty coat-collar, pulls him close, sticks his face in Swubble's and sez, now, what's your *name*, my fine fellow?

That loafer wern't spectin noffing of the sort, he's scairt. S . . . Swubble sir, he sez, all wobbly.

Evryone in the cell larfin, cheerin the doctor. Well Swubble, he sez, your name rhymes with trouble, and unless you undertake to perform a small service for me, I'll make it my business to see that trouble lies in wait for you at the prison gate the day you get out, and that it dogs your footsteps from there to the grave. D'you *believe* me, you reeking specimen of faeces?

Y . . . yessir he croaks, tho he don't know wot is this *feeseez*, and neever do I.

Good, sez the doctor, lettin go the man's collar. See this boy?

Yessir, sez, Swubble.

Stay close to him. I can tell by your demeanour you're no stranger to prison life. For the next month you will be his guide, philosopher and friend. You will protect him, speak up for him, show him what to do. If necessary you will share your miserable food with him. In short, I am making you responsible for his welfare while he remains a guest of Her Majesty. If anything unfortunate should befall him, you will answer for it on your release. If on the other hand my young friend emerges unscathed and with a favourable report as to the manner in which you carried out your duties, you will be rewarded in gold coin. Do I make myself quite clear?

Yessir, sez Swubble, but . . .

But me no *buts*, snarls the doctor. The turnkey's com

cos time's up, Doctor Snow turns to me. I'll see to it that your mother and sisters don't suffer by this Quick Nick, he sez, and I know you'll be brave. He shoots a nard glare at the loafer, then he's gone.

Clang goes that iron door, rattle goes the key; sounds wot'll drive a cove mad in time.

Nikki

There's clothes all over Demi's bed. New ones. Dresses, skirts, tops, a jacket. She picks up a little black number, shoulder-straps. Here, this one's for you.

For me? She's holding it out but I don't take it. Why me Demi? You shouldn't be buying clothes for me.

Come on. She wiggles the dress on its hanger. It's Christmas, and anyway I get a good discount for being in the trade.

Well . . . I take the garment, hold it against myself.

Just your size, yeah? She opens the wardrobe, there's a full-length mirror on the back of the door. I half-turn one way, then the other.

Yes it is. Thanks Demi, I don't know what to say.

She shrugs. Don't say anything. We're off clubbing Monday night, you can wear it then.

All of us?

God no! She shakes her head. Lads aren't invited. I see enough of them as it is. Just you and me.

Oh right. I've never been in a club. Aren't I too young?

She grins. Officially yeah but don't worry; there's ways of looking older.

I hang the dress in the wardrobe, gather my things and go along to the bathroom. When I come back, Demi's busy folding clothes into the carriers they came in. I look at her. Aren't they for you, then?

She shakes her head. I've picked out what I want, the rest're pressies for friends.

Oh. I'm feeling dead uneasy about these clothes. There must be three or four hundred poundsworth, but I've no idea how trade discounts work so I don't say anything. It's a while before I get to sleep though.

When Demi leaves next morning, the carriers go with her. When I mention it's Saturday she smiles and says, Saturday's the busiest day love, for me *and* the boys. Sure enough, it isn't long before Tan and Arrow come down. I've got coffee ready, no worries now about gas. Toast's impossible though, and when I offer to do sandwiches they claim there isn't time; they've got to be off.

No sooner have one pair gone than I hear the others moving about. Seems I'll have the place to myself today, which is lucky: I won't need to smuggle in the festive stuff I'm planning to buy.

When Monkey's stirring his coffee I say, I don't suppose there's such a thing as a toaster that works on batteries, is there?

He laughs. Not that I've heard of, Niks. Why? Missing the home comforts, are we?

No, it's not that. I thought it'd be nice for everybody to have toast and coffee in the morning, instead of just coffee.

Indeed it would milady, but there's a downside to living rent-free in a squat, and that's it. He grins. Of course, we could toast slices in front of the fire like they did in the old days, *if* you don't mind getting up at five every morning to take out the ashes, then sitting for about two hours holding a toasting-fork.

I think she *should*, says River, tipping the kettle. Just think, we'd have hot water in a morning if the fire was lit at five. Course – he smiles at me – she'd actually need to be up around four, riving out lengths of skirting board and chopping them up for fuel. *And* she'd have to do it quietly, not to disturb you and me at such an unearthly hour.

I'm getting used to their banter. I smile. Just two coffees then, eh?

Nick

I knowd coves at Sharp's Rents wot's done time in Millbank but I aint never seen inside it, nor I don't care if I never seen it agen neever. It's a place wot if I was a magistrate I won't send a *dog* to, not even a dog wot bites magistrates. In fac, if I was a magistrate I'd send a dog wot bites magistrates to the Cristal Pallis.

A nawful place. They opens up the van and hurries the nine of us down and it's a bare damp yard, no grass no weeds cos the sun's never seen inside Millbank neever. High black bildins all round, like Sharp's Rents for giants. Straitaway, turnkeys starts shovin us abowt. Firs fing, them unforchnate wimmin got to make a line by therselfs. Lady turnkeys com, clect the line of wimmin, march them acrost the yard and frou a door and I never claps eyes on 'em agen the hole monf.

Rest of us gets in line and marches frou anovver door, no fife nor drum to march to neever, jus shoves and curses. Door slams, key grinds, then they looses the manacles and we has to get undrest. I arsts Swubble, wot'll they do wiv our cloves, cos I don't want to give up my good cloff coat.

Swubble larfs, same like always. Why, he sez, they hands 'em to the manservants o'course, to be sponged and prest and mended so us'll look like dandies wen they lets us owt. He larfs agen and I knows it's not true wot he sez, but too uncomftobble naked to arst him agen.

One fat turnkey coms wiv prison cloves and we puts 'em on, stiff and hard like they made owt of waggon-covers, and the trotter-cases I gets is too big; they almos slips off of my plates wen I walks. Turnkey coms by and I sez, these boots too big for me.

He looks at me. *Sir*, he sez, you addresses me as *sir*.

These boots too big for me sir, I sez.

Makes a change, he sez, mos boys I seen in here too big for ther boots.

Millbank got miles of corriders. I aint kiddin, *miles*. We marches frou 'em, iron doors boaf sides wiv coves banged up behind 'em, but no voices. Millbank got a rule, the rule of silence they calls it, witch it meens no prisoner allowd to tork to no ovver prisoner, nor to nobody else neever. All we hears is the tramp of our boots and the ekko from it. I aint imprest wiv Millbank, I can tel you.

My heels hurtin by the time we coms to some emty cells. I spectin won cell for all of us, same like underneef the court but no, we gets won each. I never seen a cell befor. This is wot it's like: long as free men, wide as two. Stone floor, stone walls painted creem. Low, narrer stone bed wiv won straw pallet, wery fin. Won little table, won chair wot Father won't call a chair but larf and chuck it on the fire. Little little winder, bars ficker'n that pallet. One paper stuck on the back of the door witch the turnkey sez, these is the rules, can you reed?

Yes, I sez.

Yes *sir*, he sez.

Yes sir, I sez, but can't reed wery fast.

He larfs. No hurry, he sez, you got a monf. He goes out, larfin to hisself. Door clangs. Key rattles. Footsteps fades away.

Silence.

Nikki

Everyone's gone by ten. It's sleeting a bit. I check the back door's bolted and let myself out the front, locking up and putting the key in a zip-pocket with my dosh. I try the door: Demi says it's dead important to leave the place secure 'cause it's a squat. There's a sneaky wind. I turn up my collar and glance both ways, looking for Ronnie. London's a big place and he's probably not even looking for me but I've developed a horror of running into him by chance. If I have to be caught, I'd rather it was the police.

I've decided to blow my stash. I'll regret it soon enough, but at the time it seems like a reasonable thing to do. I've settled in with Demi and the dwarfs, they obviously appreciate my efforts on the domestic front so they're hardly going to chuck me out, are they? I'm grateful to them. Anybody would be in my position, and because I'm grateful I want to do something nice for them. I've got to get a present for Demi because of the dress, and you can't give to one and not the others, can you?

And there's Kirsty. Faithful Kirsty. She's bought me a present, says she doesn't expect anything from me but that's not right. No, it isn't. She's getting something whether she wants it or not. There's that CD she's been after – easy to find, easy to post. And if somebody else gets it for her, she can always take one back and change it.

I ride the tube; local shops don't stock what I'm after. I'm looking for some pre-cooked turkey meals I can heat on the stove, fancy fruits, nuts. Chocs, maybe. But before any of that, the pressies.

It takes cool to shop up west when you look like a bag lady. I tough it out, grinning up into cameras, winking at security guys in peak-caps, telling myself they take me for an eccentric billion-airess. I keep both my hands in full view at all times and I don't have a copious bag. I half expect to bump into Demi doing whatever it is she does with stock, but I don't. I don't coincide with Ronnie either, in lingerie, where I pounce on what I hope's the very thing for Demi, and he's not lurking in leather as I choose Italian belts for the lads. Relieved that part's over without my getting arrested, I pick up Kirsty's disc and head for the deli counters where I don't stick out so much.

By the time I've tracked down everything on my list, it's after twelve and I'm poor as a church mouse. I tote my bags along to a cheapo snack-shack where I can sit over a coffee and call my faithful friend.

Nick

I tel you somfing queer: a cove starts to *hear* silence wen ther's enuff of it. It coms louder'n *funder*. Swubble got the cell nex door. Won man won cell meens he can't help me like Doctor Snow telld him to, but mebbe we can tap to each ovver, break the rule of silence. My hed's so full of silence I feels it mite burst. I nocks on the wall wiv my fist. Fick wall, wery little noise but better'n noffing. I nocks agen and agen, nocks til my hand sore – but he don't nock back. I finks mebbe he don't hear, so I picks up that firewood chair and swings it at the wall. Mor noise but noffing from Swubble so I swings agen and one leg flies off, rattles acrost the floor. I starts to larf. Hit this wall wiv a chair *Father* made, wall com tumblin down. T'aint funny as all that but I can't stop larfin. I stands ther holdin my free-legged chair, larfin fit to burst. I'm larfin so much it's like cryin, witch it sounds darft but it's true.

Don't larf long tho. I don't *see* no eye at the spyhole in my door but it's ther jus the same. Firs fing I knows, the door bursts open and in coms the larfin turnkey, 'cept he aint larfin. He's holdin a long fick stave witch he swings at me, catches me upside the hed. Good larf-stopper, that stave. I seen a flash befor my eyes and falls to the floor wiv the cripple chair under me. I finks, if I stays down mebbe he won't hit me no mor, but I finks rong. He falls to beetin me abowt the sholders and back, witch it hurts somfing cronic. I raps my arms round my hed and he hits them too. I dunno how long he beets me, but jus wen I finks I'm like to die, he stops.

I knows yor sort he sez, and he's pantin like a cove wot's swum the river. I keeps my hed down. Yor one o' them *swell-mob* shavers, entcha? Finks you can larf at the rules. I stays draped over the chair, hobservin the rule of silence. Well, you got anovver fink comin, he sez. He's gettin his breff back. We gets 'em all frou here: the swells, the wiseacres, the pebbles. *Pebble*'s a cove wot'll stand a nundred lashes wivowt a sound. We gets 'em all and we *tames* 'em. He larfs. Like the month of March, evry won of 'em: coms in like lions, goes owt like lams. He larfs agen. We don't tolerate a lion at Millbank, boy, speshly a scrawny scrap of a lion like you. He prods me wiv the stave. We got a cage for yor sort; damp it is, and stinkin, pitchy-black. You'll not destroy no prison property down *ther*, my fine fellow. You'll be too busy screemin for yor poxy drab of a movver, see if you aint.

I don't like no part of Millbank but let me tel you that cell's *Buckinam Paliss* compare wiv the crib wot's waitin for me down all them slimy steps.

Nikki

'Lo Kirst.

Hi Niks, how's it hanging?

Right down the middle. I'm shopping, it's Bedlam.

It *will* be you div, last Saturday before Christmas. You up west?

Yeah, but I'm off as soon as I finish this coffee. Listen, what's your postcode?

Postcode? Why the heck . . . you haven't been spending your dosh on *me*, have you?

A little pressie Kirst, it won't break the bank.

You're an eejit. Got a pen?

Just a sec. Okay, fire away. Yes, yes, got that. It's all on this paper napkin, I'll put it into my phone later.

You're still an eejit. How's it going with the dwarfs?

Oh, they're all called Happy since *I* landed, Kirst. Clean house, sort of. Good grub, or good*ish* anyway. They're lapping it up, I feel really at home with them.

I'm glad. Just don't open the door to a crone selling apples.

Don't worry, I won't. Anything thrilling in *your* life since yesterday?

You know me Niks, never a dull moment. Now let me see, what *have* I been doing? Oh yeah, *now* it's coming back to me. I foiled a bank robbery, signed up for a trip to the International Space Station – I'll be there at the same time as Bruce Willis –

and just as I was putting the kettle on for a quiet coffee there was a knock at the door and it was flipping Robbie Williams. Could he please borrow a drop of milk, the Queen's dropped in unexpectedly and black coffee gives her heartburn.

Same old stuff then eh, Kirst?

Pretty much Niks, yeah.

Never mind. Listen, I'd better go now: place is filling up and I've nursed this cup as long as I dare. Talk to you tomorrow?

Same time. Love you, Niks.

Love you too, Kirst. Bye.

Mum?

Nikki, is that you? Where *are* you, when're you coming home? We've been frantic.

I know Mum, I'm sorry. I'm not far away but I can't come home, not while *he's* there.

Yes you *can*, sweetheart. We're not mad at you, we just want you to come home so we can sort things out. Ronnie's told me everything: how he's sometimes been a bit short with you, telling you off, and how you'd fly off the handle, yell *you're not my dad* at him, tell him he'd no right to interfere, and it's all *right*. I know it's hard for you but it's hard for Ronnie too, fitting into a ready-made family. *Please* come home for Christmas, sweetheart. Marie's pining, she doesn't understand.

It's *you*, Mum. *You* don't understand. This isn't about Ronnie telling me off, I'd never have run away over something like that. He touches me, talks dirty. He *attacked* me, Mum, came in my room and attacked me.

No he did *not*, Nikki. You're dramatizing, trying to drive a wedge between Ronnie and me because you've never liked him. Well it won't work, my girl, so you might as well . . .

I *know* – I might as well talk to a wall. Anyway I didn't call to have this conversation. I called to let you know I'll be inside a house, with friends, so don't go spoiling Marie's Christmas or your own on my account. Maybe I'll call again sometime. Bye.

Nick

Gerrup, sez the larfin turnkey, yor not hurt. I *am* hurt. He meens *he* don't feel it, and anyhow I *can*'t get up. He yells and anovver turnkey coms. They lays hands on me, pulls me to my feet.

Wher you want him, sez the ovver cove.

Down under, sez the larfin turnkey. My hart jumps cos down under's wot they calls Botny Bay:

Down under, I croaks, jus cos I breaks won poxy chair. Gets 'em larfin that does; neely larfs ther heads off.

I aint larfin. They drags me owt of the cell and on a long long corridor. I can't fink proply, evryfing hurts. Can't walk neever; my feet drags behind in them big hevvy boots. Swubble, I yells, help me, but it don't com owt a yell, mor like a croak.

Turnkey larfs. *Swubble*, he sez. Swubble wouldn't piss on his movver if she were on fire. Boaf larfin wery loud. It ekkos frou the corridor like ten lunatics.

Steps. We coms to steps goin down and they drags me, bump bump bump. Wher you takin me, I arsts. It's goin dark, we stops wile the larfin turnkey lites a candle. Takin you to yor cage, Mister Lion, he sez. Not far now.

It feels like far, bump bump bump. Steps is wet. Cold drips on my neck. That candle don't give much lite. Down we goes, down down down. I starts to fink mebbe they takin me strait to hell but suddenly no mor steps, jus this corrider like a sea cave, tho I never seen a sea cave. Can't hardly see *this* woń. We stops at a door. Iron door wot screeches wen the turnkey pulls it open. Inside it's pitchy-black and stinkin, jus like the turnkey promis. In you go, he sez, and they givs me the old heave-ho. I dives forward and sprawls full-lengf on a slimy floor.

I'm scairt. O how scairt I am jus then. The candle, I cries, leev me the candle.

No candle Mister Lion, sez the turnkey. The door screeches agen, he's shuttin it.

How long? I yells, feelin abowt me, risin to my knees.

Long enuff to turn a lion into a lam, he sez. The door slams, ther's no spyhole, candlelite gone.

I kneels ther, dursn't move, lookin wher it bin. I seen a greeny blob floatin, witch it soon fades away, takin the turnkeys' larfter and the tramp of ther boots wiv it.

I don't know even witch way is the door.

Nikki

Nobody's broken in when I get back, which is a relief. Demi and the guys're paranoid about a geezer they call the Landlord. Owns properties all over the place apparently, including this house, but not all of his properties are let. According to monkey, he snaps up run-down houses in areas he thinks'll become fashionable sometime in the future. He gets them dirt cheap and leaves 'em empty because they'd need a packet spending on them before he could put tenants in: fire-escapes, rewiring, safe boilers, carbon monoxide detectors, you name it. Empty they're costing him almost nothing, and he'll make a killing when the area goes upmarket. Monkey says speculation always involves risk, and in this instance we're *it*. I think Monkey gets off on the fact that we're gradually gutting the place in our daily quest for stuff that'll burn.

Anyway we've got away with it today. I'm first back, which is what I've been counting on. I hide the five gift-wrapped pressies on top of the wardrobe, which is one of the places I haven't got round to dusting yet. The grub I conceal behind my cleaning materials in the kitchen cupboard. This done, I light the stove, put the kettle on and start chopping veg for another stew, which I'll magic into a curry with the spices and stuff I bought from the deli.

I'll be *damned* if the smell of that native cooking doesn't come close to compensating for the nuisance of these blasted mosquitos eh, Carstairs?

Absolutely old bean, couldn't agree with you more.

Monkey and River stick their faces into the kitchen and inhale, eyes closed in rapture.

I laugh. I take it the Burra Sahibs approve?

Approve? Monkey smiles broadly. The Burra Sahibs *drool*, darling. They *squirm*. In short, it's as much as the Burra Sahibs can do to keep from uselessly expending their seed. When *is* chowtime anyway?

When the others get back.

That *long*? River groans, clutching his belly.

Never mind. Monkey drapes an arm round his friend's shoulder. The hungrier we are, the more we'll enjoy it when it *does* come. He steers River towards the front room, glances back. We'll have a pitcher of nimbu while we're waiting, girl – in the summerhouse, I think.

I tell him to go pee up a rope, which is a first for me.

Nick

I'm kneelin on cold flags, prest all round wiv black. Never seen black like this befor and I hopes never to see it agen. Black like this you *feels* it; it smovvers. Black silence is like two fick wet blankets wot you can't frow off.

I dursn't move, don't know wher anyfing is. Don't know wher the walls is, the roof, the floor. I'm giddy wiv wot I don't know. Wot if ther *aint* no walls, no roof, jus blackness goin on an on forever, witch is probly how *ded* coves feels. I finks I mus be ded and don't know it; the larfin turnkey beet me to deff.

Scairt befor, scairter now. Got to *feel* somfing: wall, bed, slop bucket, anyfing. I tries to get up, falls down. Or tries to get down falls *up*, mebbe. Oh Ma, I wisht I was home wiv you.

Wen I finks of Ma, I seen a pitcher of her and Doctor Snow, torkin at Ma's new house. That pitcher not reely *ther* o'course, but it's better'n black so I finks wery hard an gets anovver pitcher. This won's a wall in front of me. I holds it in my hed an crawls tords it and stretches owt my hand and touches it, so the black *don't* stretch forever. I turns and crawls on, feelin that wall til I feels a corner. A turn and I'm crawlin along anovver wall, feelin for a corner, witch soon com. I done two walls, lookin to feel two mor. I turns, sets off crawlin, hits agen somfing wot moves, makes a scrapin noise. I feels all round this fing and it's a bucket, witch I knowd it mus be. All this crawlin and feelin and makin pitchers got me not so scairt, tho still *pretty* scairt at that. Nex fing I feels, my bed witch it's jus stoan, no pallet. I finks of a joke Doctor Snow mite make: this lion got noffing to *lie on*, so mus be feelin better.

I coms to anovver corner, makes anovver turn. I aint felt no door yet so it mus be in this wall, witch it's number four. I shuffles along on my sore knees and shor enuff I finds it, rust comin off of it on my fingers. I don't go to that last corner, cos I won't know if the nex wall's number won agen, or number five. Don't want to feel no number five. Scairt enuff alreddy.

Nex, I have a go at standin up. The door helps me. I feels giddy for a minnit but I stands ther, won hand on the door, takin deep breffs till the giddy goes away. Then I looks round. Well, *looks* is rong o'course; wot I does is *'member*. I 'members witch way to the bed and sets off, wery slow, slidin my boots acrost the flags. It seems a long way, tho it can't be. Soon my toe hits the stoan. I bends, feels along the edge and sits down, lookin at the pitcher of the cell inside my head. Here's the bed, ther's the bucket and that way's the door. They've made me blind and dumb but can't take my pitchers away, and I can *fink* as loud as I please.

And I *won't* screem for my movver, not if they leevs me here forever.

Nikki

Nobody's brought anything Christmassy, so I'm glad I thought of it. It's after seven now, we've demolished the curry, got a decent fire going and we're sitting around with mugs of coffee, just talking. The washing-up can wait till morning, I've decided I can't be arsed struggling to do it by lamplight. These little lamps're fine for couch-potatoing – they light up our faces and leave the surrounding squalor in shadow – but they're useless to work by.

So how was business? asks Demi, looking at Monkey over the rim of her mug.

Monkey shrugs, smiles. The word *brisk* springs to mind, Demi. He looks at River. *Brisk*, would you say?

River frowns, like he's thinking. Ye-es. I reckon brisk about covers it, my son.

What is it you *do*? I've hardly spoken except to acknowledge their praise for the meal: I'm trying to join in more. Both lads glance at Demi, who responds with a small shrug.

Monkey looks at me. River and I recycle phones, Nikki.

Phones?

You know, mobiles?

Yes, but how d'you mean, *recycle*? I don't get it.

River looks up from the cigarette he's rolling. We like . . . take people's old phones off their hands so they can upgrade. It's a service really, to the public.

The penny doesn't drop till Arrow cracks out laughing. I feel a pang, I look from him to River. D'you mean . . . you *mug* people for their phones?

He lifts the cigarette, passes the paper across his tongue, smooths it down with his thumbs. That's right, darling.

But that's . . .

Dishonest? supplies Monkey. What business *isn't* dishonest, Niks? Think about it. Businesses *advertise*, right? And what's advertising but a way of misleading the public? Our product is better than theirs, this powder washes whiter than that powder, you fail as a parent if your kid doesn't have such-and-such a gismo. It's all *lies* Nikki: the products're identical and nobody needs 'em anyway. What *we* do, River and I, is exactly the same as what advertising does, which is to make sure people keep upgrading to the latest model, instead of making do with the old, unimproved version. If it weren't for us, the phone industry'd probably collapse.

They're all watching to see how I'll take it. I stare at the carpet between my toes, hearing the scrape of River's match as he lights up. They're untidy, the smokes he rolls; lumpy. He takes a drag, passes the cigarette to Monkey. Everybody's waiting.

I lift my eyes to Demi. She's finished her coffee, she's rolling the empty mug between her palms, not looking at me. Stock control, I murmur. Whose stock, Demi?

She smiles slowly, gazing at the mug. You've lived on the proceeds kiddo, received stolen goods. You're no different from the rest of us.

Yes, but *I* didn't know. I thought . . .

What? Her eyes meet mine; mocking eyes. *What* did you think, eh? That these guys were businessmen and me a career woman, dressed down, pigging it in a squat for the hell of it? She laughs. Fancy telling that to the law, do you? Think they'll believe you because you're only fourteen? I don't think so.

I don't respond straight away because there's an aching lump in my throat. I won't let them see me cry. I'm glad of the gloom as Monkey leans across to hand the rollup to Demi. When I think I've got control I say, to nobody in particular, I wasn't thinking of going to the police. I wouldn't, not after the way you've let me stay here and besides, they're looking for me. But I can't stay, not now that I know. I'd better . . . I'll go up and pack my stuff.

I nearly make it. I'm halfway out of the chair, my cheeks're dry, then I remember the pressies on top of the wardrobe, the gratitude that impelled me to choose them, and I lose it completely. The lump swells, my eyes spill over and I slump back with my face in my hands.

Nick

Forever. Feels like forever alreddy, tho I bet it aint bin more'n a hour or two. No way to tell see: no lite, no nite, no day. I sits on that hard bed, 'membrin wher is evryfing in my cell, 'membrin wot Doctor Snow sez, last fing: *I know you'll be brave.* It's cruel cold. I got my arms rapt round my body to get warm but it aint fectiv, not fectiv at all.

Fectiv's a Doctor Snow word. I'm tryin to 'member *all* the words wot he learnt me so I won't be finkin abowt the dark. *Splendid: Nick'll be splendid inside.* Don't *feel* wery splendid, and that's the troof. *Experimen, mercry, household, gainfully hemployd, laboratry.* Wisht I was in that laboratry this minnit, gainfully hemployd, but musn't fink abowt that.

Doctor Snow sez I got good *imaginayshon,* witch it's a fine fing in that laboratry or owt in the sunshine, but it aint *half* so fine in the dark. I starts to imaginate fings rite away, such as *ther's a cove in my cell: he's a lunatic and he's creepin up on me, meens to eat me cos they never feeds him anyfing else.* Darft I knows, but try tellin yorself that in the pitchy dark, the silence. Nex, my imaginayshon finks it hears footsteps owtside the cell: *turnkey comin to let me owt, they doesn't leev nobody here at nite, that's why ther's no pallet.* Ther's no lunatic o'course, jus rats scurryin abowt, an them footsteps is all inside my hed.

Time passes, I spose. I gets colder, hungrier, tireder. It'd be good to sleep. Jack always use to say, *who sleeps, eats*. Meens a cove don't feel hungry wen he's asleep, but I can't see me sleepin on a wet stoan bed, not even in my imaginayshon. Sides, I'm hopin they'll fetch som food and I don't want to miss it.

No food coms. I tel myself *it's not bin long enuff, not so long as you fink*, but it feels a wery long time. A wery, *wery* long time. I bin holdin my water, dint want to use that bucket but I'm driven to it at last. I finds it wivowt trubble, *hits* it as well, witch som coves can't do in daylite. Movin's warmd me a bit, so I goes back and forf 'tween bed an bucket countin paces, slappin my sides wiv my arms. Don't meet no lunatic, but presently I counts rong, trips over the bed and falls, scrapin my cheek down the wall. *Presently*'s anovver of them Doctor Snow words.

Tireder'n I ever bin, I lies down on that cold stoan. I don't spec to sleep, and I don't. I lies, listnin to evry little sound. *Rats and drips hobserves no rule of silence*, as Doctor Snow mite say. It don't hardly seem possible, but far into the nite or day I falls asleep. I knows I slep cos I has a dreem, witch I 'members wen I wakes.

This is my dreem: me and Jimmy o'Dowd's up at Bedlam. Ma mus be ther too cos it's her voice wot sez, they got sossidges at Bedlam, Nick. Then me and Jimmy's walkin frou a long, long corridor, iron doors boaf sides, nor Ma aint ther no mor. We coms to a room, witch it's a sort of cell. In the cell is jus won chair, and on this chair is won long fick sossidge, bigger'n any sossidge you ever seen. It's longer'n Jimmy, that sossidge. A Great Hexibishon sossidge is wot it is. Me and Jimmy's starvin. We kneels by that chair and opens our moufs, reddy to sink our teefs in the giant sossidge, but jus then won leg coms off of the chair and it tips, frowin the sossidge on the floor. The sossidge is rollin acrost the floor, me and Jimmy watchin wiv our moufs open and in trots the larfin turnkey wiv his stave, witch he starts to beet us wiv it, and that's wen I wakes up.

I knows it's bin a dreem but I can *smell* that sossidge. I even feels abowt for it, but all I finds is a pan of cold skilly som turnkey slided frou a hatch in my door.

Nikki

We're the same *people*, Niks. Nothing's changed, just 'cause you know where the dosh comes from. Demi's kneeling at the side of the chair, one arm across my shoulders. I wriggle, trying to shake her off.

I went out, I sob. Bought stuff – turkey, pressies. I thought you were my *friends*.

We *are*, sweetheart. This from River. We care about you. You've made everything so much better in just a few days.

Yes, but I *wouldn*'t have, not if I'd known. Don't you see, I was in the *right*. Now I'm as much a criminal as that Ronnie.

Was Snow White a miner? goes Demi.

What?

Snow White. She wasn't a miner was she, just 'cause the dwarfs were. She kept house.

It's not the *same* though is it, I murmur. Mining's legal, and anyway that's just a fairy story. It isn't *right*, what you lot do. I can't be part of it.

All right darling, smooths Monkey. You're right about us, we're no good, but it's Christmas in two days. If you go now it'll mean spending it on the street, with everything shut and everybody gone, and it's absolute hell. I know because I've done it, and I damn near threw myself in the river.

He's telling the *truth*, Niks. Demi's got both arms round me now. Say you'll stay, at least till after the holiday. Then, if you really want to leave we won't try to stop you. Okay?

I don't *want* to give in, I really don't, but what Monkey said has got to me. It was bad enough sleeping rough when there were people about and places I could nip into for a pee and a coffee and a warm. The thought of being out there alone with every door locked against me's just too horrifying, especially now I've spent most of my dosh. What a plonker I was to do that. I nod, despising myself. All right, but just till the holiday's over.

Good girl, says Demi. Here. She hands me a wodge of stolen Kleenex, I blot my cheeks and blow like I'm seven years old. She nods and smiles. Who's Ronnie, by the way?

Nick

I'm in that hole a week. A
week, on greasy skilly I never seen. Don't *never* eat grub
you can't see, it don't half spoil the happetite. I don't *know*
it's bin a week; feels like I done the hole *monf* wen they
takes me owt. Finks they *dischargin* me: All them corriders
looks the same and I can't see much anyhow, lite hurtin
my eyes, but we stops at last and I rekernize the cell I
has befor. 'Ere we are, sez the larfin turnkey, back at
yor hotel. He's dispointed cos I dint screem in the dark,
dint beg. He don't know how close I com to it, a fousand
times.

How long? I arst.

Reserved for free weeks yor highness, he sez, but we
can arrange a long *hextenshon* if you sheds that lam's fleece,
turns into a lion agen. He opens up, shoves me in. Clang
goes the iron door, rattle goes the key.

Don't plan to be a lion no mor. Not in here. Won week
in pitchy dark's long enuff for Nick, but jus wait til I'm
owt. Treet a cove like a hanimal and he *coms* a hanimal. I
meens to make 'em sorry.

This is wot I finks, firs day back in my cell. Second day
too, as I sits pickin the oakum they keeps us busy wiv.
Oakum's tarry old rope off of ships. We has to pick it apart
so they can make new ropes from it. Don't sound hard if

you never done it, but yor fingers bleeds after a day or two and it hurts just to hold that stiff black rope, never mind pick. I've heard it said that hardend convicts'll weep pickin oakum, and I can bleev it.

Worse'n the oakum's the rule of silence. A cove needs to hear ovver coves, and be heard by 'em. Sounds like noffing, that rule of silence, but men have gon mad under it, wimmin too. Can't even get a word owt of the turnkey wot fetches the oakum, carries it away, brings the skilly. Nice day, you sez wen he coms in, but he jus picks up the basket, rummages frou to see you done it rite and goes owt. It's as if you aint even *there*, and after a wile you starts wondrin yorself: am I noffing, nobody? Cruel barsets invented the rule of silence and cruel barsets enforces it, and that's the troof.

And then ther's the wittles. Bread and skilly, bread and skilly, day after day after day. It's such poor stuff, even if you bin hungry all of yor life you gets sick at the site and smell of it after a wile. Gets so a cove can't fink abowt noffing 'cept grub, nor dreem of anyfing else at nite. Years later, I talks wiv a old convict wot use to dreem evry nite of feastin on hot roast turnkey, served wiv onion gravy. I only done a monf in my life, but I knowd zacly how that old man felt.

Wot saved me, the won fing wot stopt me settin off on a life of crime wasn't prison, it was Doctor Snow's wondrous words. They'd kept me from madness in that dungeon, and now they workt their magic as I sat pickin oakum wiv sore fingers and a sick belly. If I'd went into Millbank wivowt them words I'd've com owt hardend, took to crime, probly choked owt my life on the gallows by and by. As it was I com owt resolved to be like the Doctor, to make him proud of me.

Nikki

Who *is* Ronnie, Niks?

They're watching me again. I stuff the balled-up tissues in my pocket, sniff and sigh. He's my mum's boyfriend.

Ah. Demi nods. The old old story, eh?

What you *on* about? goes Tan.

Demi looks at him. The old old story, knucklehead: *mum falls for some guy, brings him home to meet the kids, guy doesn't see kids, he sees a gorgeous teenage girl who's fair game 'cause they're not related; guy moves in with mum, starts pestering daughter, daughter tells mum who doesn't believe her 'cause she's besotted with the guy; situation gets heavier and heavier, daughter moves out.* Is that how it went, Niks?

I nod, looking at the floor. The dwarfs murmur.

So this guy, says Monkey, exhaling smoke, this Ronnie, he was messing around with you, yeah?

Yes.

And you told your Mum and she wouldn't believe you?

No, she wouldn't.

Did you think about Childline, the police?

Oh yes, I thought about everything, but the only thing I could do without getting Mum into trouble was run off.

Don't you have rellies? asks Arrow. An auntie or a gran you could go to?

I've got a dad, but he's with somebody else. My gran thinks

I'm a slag who came on to Ronnie, and my Auntie's a snooty cow in West Sussex.

So which of 'em will you try when you leave here? This from River.

I shake my head. I dunno, probably none of them. I'll go back where Demi found me.

Nobody comes back to me on this. Demi pats my shoulder and goes back to her seat. River crushes the spent rollup in a takeout tray, fishes a nugget of resin from his pocket, strikes a match and holds one end of the nugget in the flame. I gaze across at Tan till I catch his eye. What about you and Arrow, Tan. What service to the public do *you* perform?

His mouth warps in a wry smile. My partner and I are in banking, Nikki.

Shouldn't that be *un*banking, mate? amends Arrow.

You . . . rob banks?

Tan chuckles. Not the way *you* mean love. Not the Bonnie and Clyde method. Heard of card surfing, have you?

No.

Oh, well, that's what me and Arrow do. Basically it's collecting pin numbers, acquiring the cards that go with them and making withdrawals. Manual dexterity's the key to it – that and speed. He grins. The bike helps with the speed.

Arrow's expression is pained. Don't look like that sweetheart. Beauty of our job is, nobody suffers. Card company reimburses the cardholder, insurers pay the card company, policyholders pick up the tab for the insurers without realizing it. Everyone's happy.

I shake my head. The dosh must come from *somewhere*.

Oh it *does* Niks. Ultimately, it comes from where *all* dosh comes from: the taxpayer.

He's right Nikki, supports Monkey. Ask yourself this: if you were a taxpayer, which would you rather they spent your contributions on – keeping a pair of harmless layabouts like Tan and Arrow, or paying the salaries of two guys in uniform who fly a jet that drops bombs on villages, killing and maiming kids who've never hurt anyone?

I . . . I'd rather do neither.

Ah, but that's not an option Niks. My question was *which*, if you had to choose?

I shrug, pull a face. The layabouts, I suppose.

Of course! Nobody in his right mind would choose kid-killers over harmless dropouts, so there you go. Here. He leans across, hands me River's new rollup. Have a toke on this; it'll clear your mind.

Nick

Free weeks feels like free monfs: it rolls round, but I'm wery glad I dint get a year like Swubble. One mornin early they marches me back frou all them corriders, givs me my own cloves and puts me owt the gate and Bob's yer uncle.

The sun's shinin, sparrers is twitterin. I stands ther, breevin. Ther's no wevver in clink, same evry day; a cove don't know fings're changing owtside. It's warmer, briter, even here at Millbank, witch aint zacly Hamton Court you mite say. Best fing of all is, no doors is slammin, no keys is rattlin.

I'm standin ther, jus breevin, finkin abowt Ma and the little gels, as how we'll all be togevver in won hour, wen a gig pulls up acrost the road and Doctor Snow gets down. I'm happy to see the doctor but I knows he aint com for me: gentlemen doesn't clect felons in gigs. Must be makin a call nearby.

He seen me tho, makes to crost. I smiles and he givs a little nod but no smile, and that's wen I knows somfing's rong. Doctor . . . I sez, as he coms close.

Nick, he sez. Oh, my poor Nick. He grasps my sholders and draws me tord him, then somfing tels me wot it mus be.

I pulls back, looks at him. It's Ma, I sez. Somfing's happend to Ma.

He don't say noffing, jus nods.

I grasps *his* sholders and he don't knock my hands away. *Wot?* I cries. Wot is it, sir?

There's cholera, he sez, at Golden Square and all about. Your mother . . . I *tried* to see you Nick, to tell you before she . . . He jerks his head tord the prison gate. They wouldn't admit me: your mother succumbed very early this morning.

Ma . . . Ma's *ded*, sir? My lovely Ma, whose hart I break wen I goes to prison?

He shakes his hed. You didn't break your mother's heart Nick. She was proud of you. If she'd been spared one more day she'd have told you so herself.

The *gels*, I sez. My little sisters, who's carin for *them*?

Your mother cared for them Nick, he sez, and his voice is wery gentle, till they had no further need of care.

At Sharp's Rents I fort I had noffing, but I was rong. *Now* I has noffing. Nick was a son and a brovver, now he's a horfan. Better by far they'd left him to the pitchy dark, in the emtiness of time.

Nikki

Christmas is good, considering. I think my pressies're a success. It doesn't feel as nice as it would have if I hadn't found out about Demi and the dwarfs, but still. The grub's good in a boil-in-the-bag sort of way, we manage to get the front room quite warm and River's lumpy rollups make me mellow to the point of sentimentality: I get all tearful on the phone, tell Kirsty I'd rather be here than anywhere else on earth.

We'd had a good time Christmas Eve, Demi and me, which put me in the right mood. Pullit, the club was called, and the D J was Moby Disc. The doormen – Demi called them Saint Peters – knew her, so there was no problem about letting me in. The beat was fantastic, and there were some gorgeous lighting effects. I'd never been on a dance floor before, expected to feel really self-conscious but in fact I was into it straight away, me and my little black dress. We danced ourselves out then retired to the chillout room and a bunch of lads followed, insisting on buying us drinks. I said I didn't drink and this lad brought me a Red Bull. Demi said it was just pop so I drank it, but I think there must've been something in it because I started acting really stupid, flicking coasters into people's laps and laughing like a loony. It was late when we left, and I seem to remember Demi had a hard time shaking the lads off so they wouldn't get in our taxi.

Anyway Christmas Day is fine, and we stay in bed most of

Boxing Day – easiest way to keep warm. I drift in and out of sleep, vaguely aware that I'd better make the most of the comfy bed while I've got it, because tomorrow night I'll be on the street. In dream fragments I'm out there already, huddled in the doorway of a dark, silent Pullit, hungry and bursting to pee.

I think I know, even half-asleep, that I'll weaken and stay when it comes to it.

Nick

They frowd 'em in a pit, my fambly. A *pit*. The fambly of Daniel Webley the carpenter, brung low by misforchune but workt therselfs up and was never a charge on the Parish.

Doctor Snow shows me this pit. He don't want to but I has to see it, say farewell. They frowd *me* in won too, I sez, my voice full of weepin. They finks if they keeps a wicked cove in the dark for a time, he'll com owt a virtuous cove.

Ignorance Nick, sez the doctor. Ignorance is the enemy. We must work to conquer ignorance till, little by little, hatred and superstition fade away to be replaced by compassion and commonsense. Till the prison cell and the penal colony are rendered redundant by the enlightenment which will usher in an age of social justice.

Fousand Doctor Snow words floats acrost that pit. I hears 'em but can't take 'em in. My hed too full wiv greef. Wen I stands silent he sez, oh Nick, all this seems nothing to you now, words, empty as graveside prayers, but there's a difference, which is this: the promises made in prayers can never be redeemed by the mightiest strivings of mankind, while those I speak of lie well within the compass of our capabilities. Courage will be needed. Courage and commonsense and work, work, work. For our part Nick, yours and mine, the work is already in hand. Thanks largely to the loved ones who lie sleeping in this earth we shall conquer cholera, for the circumstances of their demise have pointed out the way.

. I don't unnerstan all wot the doctor sez, but knows that he meens to be kind. Wants me to bleev Ma and the little gels died for somfing, not noffing. They ded tho, I got to bleev that. Evryfing else mus wait til anovver time. Anovver time.

Nikki

Thursday morning Demi's like, you off today then? We're not even *up* and she's on my case.

Uh? Squinting across the dark bedroom I can just make her out, propped on one elbow, watching me. Something's lashing the window, trying to get in. Sounds like sleet. Oh yeah, I mumble, gimme half an hour.

She snorts. You deaf Niks or what? Can't you *hear* it out there? She means the weather.

Course I can hear it. I start getting out of bed, room's like a fridge.

It's bloody *freezing*, you moron. Have you thought what it'll feel like, sitting on stone in some doorway on a day like this? A whole *lot* of days like this? Relax for Pete's sake, nobody's kicking you out.

Sitting on the bed with my feet on cold boards, I pause. I'd like to claim I'm wrestling with my conscience but I'm not. I'm waiting to be persuaded that's all, so it won't look like an instant cave-in. Demi probably knows this. Look, she says, you can't run away from home at fourteen and expect to stay pure as the driven snow. You've got to eat, got to keep warm, got to *hussle*. It's not your fault, it's the hand you were dealt, you can only play it. Get back into bed, snuggle down and have a nice long snooze. Let the *wind* worry about driven snow.

I'm back in my nest, feeling pathetic, before her head hits

the pillow. Pathetic but warm. I should've gone I know, but I'm weak; too weak to face the street. I lie curled like a foetus, reviewing my options.

Dad. I could phone Dad I suppose, but what about this Laura character, this *solicitor*? Sounds like a stuck-up bitch to me. Don't rate my chances of hitting it off with her at all. Cuckoo in the nest is what I'd be up there in Yorkshire.

Okay, so what about Steve Patten, sensitive, considerate Steve with his nice flat in Bermondsey? I'm pretty sure he'd let me stay; *said* so didn't he, but would it be fair? He's a *Big Issue* vendor, which means he's been through some sort of a bad patch and he's trying to get his life back on track. He might be glad of the company, but being saddled with a fourteen-year-old runaway's hardly going to help him back into the mainstream, is it? He's such a fantastically good guy, I'd never forgive myself if he ended up being prosecuted for harbouring me. So no.

Which leaves what? Auntie Steph in Sussex by the sea. I hardly know my Auntie Steph. She's Mum's sister but they're not close. She used to send birthday pressies when I was little, still sends them to Marie, but I've only seen her about three times in my life. I can't turn up there and ask to be kept, even if I had her address, which I don't.

Cross off Auntie Steph, and there's just the street.

I must've fallen asleep then, because the next thing I know it's light and Demi's standing over me with a steaming mug in her hand. She smiles. Monkey says if you let him have your phone till tonight, he'll get it charged up.

Nick

I resumes my duties at Pulteney Court. There's no necessity Nick, sez Doctor Snow. Take time to mourn your dead. Time has the cure for what's hurting you.

I won't contradic the doctor but I feels better wiv somfing to do, so I fetches and carries and sweeps like before, and he don't stop me. He's such a toff to me, Doctor Snow: done more for me than any gentleman ever done for a cove before in the hole world. Gives me a upstairs room for my own, pays my wages, teeches me to write and read and cipher. I was nothing but a hurchin when I come here, but he treets me like a son.

One day, when time's bin healing me a little bit, he tells me about the Broad Street pump. That's where the cholera was, Nick, he says. In the water that came from the Broad Street pump. Everybody who caught the cholera while you were at Millbank, including your dear Ma and the little girls, had drunk water drawn from that pump. It was the only thing they had in common, and that's how I knew. And that's what I meant when I said your loved ones pointed out the way. In a few tragic days, those poor souls disposed of bad air theory *and* any lingering notion of divine retribution. Dirty water causes cholera, Nick, and clean water will rid us of it.

It helped me, knowing my family dint die for nothing: they died so thousands mite live. It helped me a lot.

One day, out about the doctor's business, I come by Jack's pitch. If I'd have been thinking I might have chosen another way, cos Jack probly didn't know about Ma and I still weren't happy talking about it.

I'm walking in a sort of daydreem when I hears a loud and familiar voice. Old mates not good enuff for you eh, since you bin a toff? I looks across and there's good old Jack, standing by his cart in the sunshine. I makes my way over, shoving through the crowd. Master Nicholas, he larfs, on his way to Fred Needle Street to count his gold, I'll bet. It's clear he hasn't heard about my bereevment.

Jack! We shakes hands. How's things with you? Bet continues well, I hopes?

Bet's in rude elf Nick, an so am I, fank the lord. Wot about yourself?

Oh, I'm carrying on all right Jack, thank you for arsking.

He looks at me. *Somfing's* not rite old son, it's in yer voice.

So out it comes, with many a tear. Jack's a good old friend, listens to everything, then puts his arm round my sholders and hands me a big red kerchif to wipe my cheeks. I dries my eyes, offers it back. Naw, he says, shaking his head. You 'ang on to it son; too grand for me anyhow. He looks at me. Wot I done Nick, he says, yellin out like that when I seen you, wouldn' a done it if I'd've knew . . .

I *knows* Jack, it's all right. I gives him a smile, my first for a long time. I'd better scud along. Doctor'll think me knocked down by a waggon.

All right son, he says, mind how you go. Stop by and see your old mate sometimes, eh?

I'm glad I didn't choose another way. Feels better for talking to Jack. Doctor Snow notices wen I gets back to Pulteney Court. Is it my imagination Nick, he says, or are you perking up just a little?

I nods. I seen Jack, sir. Jack Kaggs, the coster.

Ah. He nods. Friends: they're a great blessing, especially in times of sadness. He looks at me. Do you miss that life Nick? Costering, I mean?

No sir, I says, I misses Ma. That life was good cos she was in it. I'm satisfied with my present sitivation, sir.

Are you, Nick? He smiles. It's not much of a life though, for a bright young fellow like you. I've been wondering . . .

I looks at him. He don't usually break off like that. What sir? I arsks.

Whether it might not be a good thing if you could get away, Nick. *Right* away. Make a fresh start, far from dirt and squalor and sad memories.

I smiles. Sad memries *wherever* I goes sir, I says.

Oh yes I *know* Nick, I didn't mean . . .

Where sir? I arsks. Where could I go, cove like me, been to prison? Nobody offers a sitivation to a man who's been to prison.

He nods. That's exactly what I mean, Nick. Here, your past will haunt you, hold you back. But suppose you were in a place where nobody knows about Sharp's Rents, Millbank, the baked potato man. A place where people would look at you and see only a strong, bright lad, willing and able to turn his hand to anything?

I smiles. Why sir, I say, if there was such a place, Quick Nick'd go there tomorrer.

Would he? Would he *really*, Nick? arsks the doctor.

Like a shot sir, I tell him.

Well Nick, he says, there *is* such a place, and if you want me to I'll speak with a lady of my acquaintance who is able to arrange passages for young persons like you.

Passages, sir?

Aye lad, passages: to New South Wales.

My heart sinks. I knows a *cove* who arranges them passages sir, I say. I calls him the Larfing Turnkey.

Nikki

She hands me the coffee, sits down on the edge of my bed. It's only half-light outside. There's just the one lamp on top of the wardrobe; it illuminates one side of her face.

So, have you decided?

Time is it?

Half-eight and chucking it down. You're not *really* going to pack your stuff and move out, are you? At least wait till the weather picks up a bit.

I snort. When'll *that* be, Demi – April, May?

She shrugs. Probably.

I shrug too. Okay, I'll stay if it's all right with everyone, but I'm not getting into nicking, allright? I'll shop, cook, clean; I won't steal. And yes, I'll give Monkey my phone.

Fine. She stands up. I'm off: January sales actually start in December, you know. Lads'd probably appreciate a spot of breakfast, morning like this. See you.

So that's it. I'm maid of all work in a houseful of scallies. I keep telling myself Snow White wasn't a miner, but the last of my dosh has gone and deep down I know that if you live on scally earnings, you're a scally.

The weather stays foul over New Year and all through January. Arrow finds one of those old push-along carpet sweepers in a skip – at least he *says* it was in a skip. It's a Ewbank so we call it Chris. The threadbare carpet in the front room looks almost presentable once I've gone over it a few times, though I don't think it would in full daylight.

Now that I know the score, the lads don't mind talking about their work, and I learn a bit more about card-surfing. How it works is, one of them hangs about near some cash machine on Oxford Street or wherever there are rich tourists. When someone comes to draw cash, he watches them enter their pin number and puts it in his mobile phone, in the memory. He's not interested in the cash, it's the card he wants. His partner, lurking nearby, has noticed where the tourist keeps the card. It's often in a backpack, which makes the job that much easier. He follows the tourist and lifts the purse or wallet containing the card, usually while the victim is waiting with a bunch of others to cross the road. Meanwhile the other partner has collected the bike and is wheeling it along the pavement. He's put on a skid-lid so people think he's one of those messengers. Nobody connects the two partners. As soon as the pickpocket has the wallet, he brushes past the cyclist and hands it to him. The cyclist wheels his machine round a corner, mounts up and rides off at speed while his partner merges with the crowd. That way, if the pickpocket has been spotted by a policeman on a CCTV monitor, he's carrying nothing incriminating when he's accosted. Meanwhile the cyclist takes a convoluted route to a cash machine a few streets away, makes a single large withdrawal using the digits in the phone, throws away the card and rides off.

Simple, isn't it? But it's a masterpiece of sophistication compared to what Monkey and River do, which is to spot some kid using a bang up-to-the-minute phone and take it from him or her, using violence where necessary.

And Demi shoplifts.

*

People who've had a fairly normal upbringing tend to wonder how people *get* like that; what makes some people decide to rob, rather than get jobs like everybody else. I don't know the answer of course, but having shared a home with Demi and the dwarfs I can say this: none of them's evil, whatever that's supposed to mean. None of them's a beast or a monster or a fiend, or any of the other names the tabloids put in big black headlines so their readers needn't strain themselves wondering what actually causes crime. Somewhere along the line, something goes wrong for the Demis, the Monkeys, the Tans, and we need to know what, because until we track down the cause, we haven't a snowball in hell's chance of finding a cure.

It's the same with a disease, innit?

Nick

The doctor larfs. No no Nick, he says, I'm talking about emigration, not transportation.

Ah, I says, cos one of them words is new to me. I thought as I heard you say *New South Wales*, sir.

He nods. I mentioned New South Wales Nick, but I wasn't referring to the penal colony. Many people have gone out there as free settlers. It's called emigration, and more are setting out even as we speak, because there's space in New South Wales, acre upon acre of good, fertile land which nobody owns. There are no slums, Nick, no festering cesspits, no contaminated water, no cholera. A man who is prepared to work hard can save money and buy land, clear it, make a farm out of it. Imagine: your own farm, a house as big as you like, pure clean air to breathe and people working for you. D'you think you'll ever have those things here in England, Nick?

Oh *yes* sir, I jokes. I expects to come a Squire, dine on wenison and hunt with the 'ounds, all in my cell at Bedlam o'course.

He larfs. You're coming back to yourself, Nick, which pleases me no end. He looks at me. So what d'you say? Shall I speak to my acquaintance?

Before I knows it I've said yes. T'were no more than a

week ago, and now here I am in my room at Pulteney Court with a bag packed, ready for the off. I'm to be one of a party sent away by something called The Children's Friend Society, to New South Wales. I tells them I has a bit of carpentry from Father so they're sending me without training me first, Lord help me. Mebbe if I puts this London far behind, I won't be forever seeing Ma across the street; won't hear little girls weeping.

Nikki

There's been a guy here asking after you, says Tan. It's eleven in the morning, first Saturday in February. I've been down the swimming baths for a shower. I place a chair in front of the fire and drape my towel over the back to dry. I'm acting cool while panicking inside.

Police, was he? I've been expecting the police since the day I moved in.

Tan shakes his head. Don't think so. I assumed he was from the landlord, wouldn't let him in, so we shouted through the door. I reckon if he'd been a copper he'd have given me a harder time.

What did he look like?

Tan pulls a face. Mid-thirties, five-tennish, slim. He'd a long mac and one of those tweedy check hats with a little feather in the band, you know the sort of thing. Oh, and a little sandy moustache. The word *prat* sprang to mind.

Ronnie. I thought I'd said it to myself, but I must've spoken the name out loud because Tan nods.

That'd be about right, Niks. How the heck d'he trace you *here*?

You didn't *tell* him I live here, did you?

Course not, what d'you take me for? Said I didn't know anyone by the name of Minton.

And what did he say?

200

Said you'd been seen coming in and out, you or some-body like you. I'm not satisfied, he said. I'll be back. Then he walked off.

Oh God! I slump in an armchair. How long ago was this, Tan? I could've walked right into him.

'Bout twenty minutes. What could he do if he *did* run into you, Niks? If I was him, finding you'd be the *last* thing I wanted. You can put him inside just by opening your mouth.

I shake my head. I dunno Tan, but I've been dreading bump-ing into him ever since . . . He said he'd be back?

Yes, but I wouldn't get paranoid about it. It's the sort of thing people say, then you never see 'em again. Anyway, all you've got to do is stay in for a bit and keep the door locked. The rest of us'll do the shopping, and if you've absolutely *got* to go out, one of us'll go with you. All right?

Yes. I suppose I knew somebody'd track me down sooner or later, but it's still a shock.

Sure it is. Here: have one of River's smokes. I'll put the kettle on for when the others get back.

Nick

I am genuinely sorry to be losing you Nick, says Doctor Snow. The two of us is stood by the foot of the gangplank of the *New Venture*, the three-master that'll carry me and two hundred other settlers to New South Wales, or perhaps to the bottom of the sea. I'm sorry to be leaving the Doctor, and now it's come to it I'm so afraid I feels like pulling out; arsking for my sitivation back. Doctor Snow seen this in my face. It's a long way, Quick Nick, he says, and it'll all seem wondrous strange at first, but you're strong, bright and willing, and you'll make your way, I know you will.

Yessir, I says, and I takes up my bag with the strong clothes inside wot he's given me. Coves're clomping up the gangway, coves and women, and someone's shouting up on deck. There's an aching lump in my throat; if I goes to say more I'll cry, which aint the best start to a great adventure. I turns and hurries up the plank with my bag, feeling the doctor's eyes on my back.

On deck, I shoves to get a place at the rail. He's still there, looking up. I waves and he waves back, shouts, don't forget to write. I still got the lump so I nods, smiles. He smiles too, then turns and leaves the quayside, pushing through the crowd. I cries then, cos thinking in bed last night I seen a picture of the ship moving out, Doctor Snow on the keyside coming littler and littler but waving still, me waving back, til we can't see each other no more. Course I knows he's busy, got the cholera on the run, but still I wished it might have bin more like my picture.

I goes below, gets my sleeping space, which aint very big at that. Dark and low down here, surprised to see women and nippers and men, all in together. I sits on my space to keep it, but when they feels the ship move everyone rushes up on deck to catch the last of London, and I goes too. If Ma and the little girls were standing on the shore this minute, I'd throw myself overboard and try to swim to them, though I never swimmed before. As it is I feels sad and scared, but I finds I can bear it. And so I leaves England, nor I don't expect to see it ever again, not even in the fullness of time.

There's coves on board wot's worse off than me. Eighty convicts, some transported for life. Us free settlers never seen their space, but we hears it's lower and darker than ours, and their grub's even worse, though that's hard to imagine – and they're shackled as well, night and day. As we sails south and things gets worse and worse, I keeps thinking on them miserable coves and reminding myself I'm one of the lucky ones.

Soon we runs into rough weather and our space stinks worse than Sharp's Rents, everybody's sick and not enough slop buckets. There's no sleep neither, not with nippers howling, women screeching and coves forever scrapping over space and thiefing off of one another. Many a night I lies crammed in my damp, stinking space, wishing it mite be my grave. Nine days out a nipper dies and is buried at sea, and a few days after, we hears that a convict, brung on deck to be flogged, breaks free and chucks hisself over the side, nor I don't reckon they wastes much time looking for him neither.

South, south we sails, and by and by it comes wery hot, hotter than I'd ever have believed. The sailors leaves the hatch-cover off all night but still we can't hardly breathe. To keep their spirits up, coves is forever talking about the gold wot's been found in Australia, and how *they* means to find some and be rich. By now everyone knows some of us'll never live to see New South Wales, let alone gold, but there's no turning back so no point thinking about it.

New Venture calls in at a few ports to take on water and wittles. We crowds the rail to buy fruit off of dusky coves in little boats, and to look at land, but we're not let ashore in case we bring plague, and cos we don't bring money. After a time there's no more ports, no more fruit, no fresh water. Sickness thrives in the damp and heat below. There's more and more burials at sea. I catch myself wishing I was walking by the frozen Thames, or even in that black, black Millbank dungeon.

If you wonders what *forever* feels like, sail to New South Wales.

Nikki

Hi Kirst.

Half-twelve. I'm over the first shock; talking to Kirsty'll make it better.

Nikki, sorry but I've got your mum here. She needs to talk, don't hang up.

Kirsty . . .

Nikki?

What d'you *want*, Mum? I suppose it was you sent Ronnie snooping round?

You haven't *seen* Ronnie, have you? I don't want him anywhere near you.

Huh, *that*'s a new one. Had a tiff or something?

No, *listen* sweetheart, *please*. I *know* about him now, you were telling the truth. I'm sorry I didn't believe you.

You know? How d'you know?

I found him with your sister.

With *Marie*? But she's only . . .

Seven, I know. He's gone, I threw him out. Listen: I've been to the police, they're looking for him, there'll be a case. I need you to tell them about you and Ronnie. Come home sweetheart. There's nothing to stop you now.

Is *Kirsty* listening to all this, Mum?

No, she left the room but she knows, more or less.

Oh, God! Put her on, will you?

Come home, talk to her face to face.

I don't know if I *can*, Mum. It's not the sort of thing . . .

Just come *home*, it'll sort itself out.

It's not that simple, Mum. I've got friends here, they took me in, I can't just walk out on them.

I *know*, Nikki. I understand about your friends. I *owe* them, but there's nothing to stop you keeping in touch from home, is there?

Yes there *is*, Mum. You don't know them, what sort of people they are. If you did, you wouldn't want me having anything to do with them. It's another *world* I'm in, that's what you don't understand.

I do understand. I *do*. I promise I won't try to stop you seeing anybody you want to see, if you'll only come home. Say you will, sweetheart, *please*.

I dunno Mum, I'm all confused. Stuff's happening too fast. Listen. I'll talk to my friends, call you later. Tomorrow, probably. Okay?

Well, I can't say no can I, if that's what you're going to do, but you mentioned Ronnie snooping?

He came knocking. I was out.

Yes, well I don't know what he's playing at but you be careful, d'you hear? Don't talk to him, don't let him near you.

Don't worry, I won't. There's guys here'll soon see him off if he comes bothering me. I'll catch you later okay?

Yes, and I'm sorry Nikki love. About everything.

Yes, well . . .

Nick

Land Ho! A sailor shouts this when Australia comes in sight. You'd expect that everyone would rush up on deck, but most of us are too sick to bother. Besides, we knows by now how tedious slow the time goes between sighting land and lying alongside.

The ship ties up at Sydney though, in the fullness of time. Somebody yells down the hatch for us to shake a leg and we rouses up, starts getting our bags together. Two hundred of us left London, one hundred and eighty-one lives to clap eyes on Sydney.

I'm disappointed by Sydney. Doctor Snow told me Australia would be wide and green, plenty of space for everyone, but this Sydney's a city much like London. All over houses, horses, carts; people all crushed together, pushing and shouting. Stinks as well probably, but the *New Venture* stinks far worse so we don't notice.

Long time til they lets us on that gangplank, gangplank we all bin dreaming about for weeks past. But they lets us go at last and here's a queer thing: we've bin talking about *terra firma*, which is scholard for firm ground, but when we sets foot on this *terra* it don't feel *firma* at all; it seems to move under our boots like the ship. Maybe Australia's *afloat*, says one wag.

We're standing there beside the pile of our bags, feeling

relieved and afraid at the same time, wondering what will happen next, when they brings the convicts off. I seen some pitiful sights in London, but I never seen humans look so much like beasts. Thin they are, and pale; dead-eyed and caked with filth. They shuffles down the gangplank all in chains, and before they's hardly set foot on land here's soldiers, shouting and cursing and pushing 'em in line. The stink coming off of 'em's something vile, and I thank God I'm not a convict, sick and apprehensive though I am. We watches the soldiers march the poor wretches away. *I don't care what they done*, says a woman sofly, *they aint hardly deserved this*.

It's hot just standing. I don't want to think what it'll be like *working*. A cove near me arsks, is that the same sun we has in London? He don't get no answer cos nobody knows. I expect they *got* scholards in Australia, just not on this particular dock.

Nikki

Saturday night is takeaway night. It's the only time we have a proper cooked meal really. It's also the one time I can share something the guys fetch in without wondering if it's nicked. It's bought with the proceeds of crime I know, but I can kid myself it's legit.

We eat, sit back, belch contentedly. Bits of back room floor burn brightly on the hearth. A joint circulates, the first of many. Even scallies deserve Saturday night. It's a shame Tan has to spoil it. Nikki's got something to tell us, he says.

It's not heavy, I assure them. I've had a couple of tokes, nothing's heavy. I gaze around from the depths of my armchair. Their faces are pale blobs in the gloom. It's just, I had my Mum on the phone. She wants me home.

She always *has*, hasn't she? asks Demi.

Well yeah, but it's different now. I tell her about Ronnie and my little sister. He's gone, you see. I'd never go home while he was there, but she's chucked him out.

He was here, adds Tan. This morning, asking for Nikki. She was out.

I nod. Yes, and he said he'd be back. I don't know what he wants, but Mum says I'm not to let him near me, so . . .

I know what he wants. This from Arrow. I look at him.

Well it's obvious, isn't it? Your mum caught him committing a serious offence. She'll have told the police and they're after

209

him. At his trial, he might manage to convince a jury he was just giving the little lass a cuddle or something, but with you as a star witness he'll have no chance. I reckon he's out to make sure you won't be there.

You mean he's planning to *kill* me? Bit melodramatic, isn't it?

Arrow's got the spliff. He draws deeply on it, passes it to Demi, exhales slowly. His voice issues from the midst of a cloud. Not really, not when you know what happens to guys like him inside. I think *I'*d consider murder in his position.

Oh *shit*, Arrow. I feel scared suddenly. That's the *last* thing I'd have thought of.

Suppose the guy *is* after bumping you off, says Tan. Where d'you think you'd be safer: here with us or at home with your mum?

I . . . I dunno, Tan. I suppose I'd *feel* safer at home, 'cause of the bright lights and locking windows and that, and because I wouldn't be by myself all day like I am here, but . . .

But what?

Well – you've all been so nice to me, I can't just *go* the minute I don't need you anymore.

Why not? asks Monkey. *I* would. Any of us would. We haven't been *nice* at all. We needed a serving wench.

*I'*ve been nice, protests River. I'm always nice, and Nikki's *much* more than a serving wench to me. Anyway you can't go tonight Niks: he might be out there. Sunday tomorrow, decide then, eh?

I nod as Demi hands me the inch-long joint. I draw, inhale. Okay then, tomorrow it is. Here, Tan. I pass the butt, lie back and close my eyes. My memory exhales a skein of song: . . . *tomorrow's far away, in the air*.

Spot on every time, those seventies songwriters.

Nick

Feels like an age, standing on that quay. Presently a cove goes to try to find out what we're supposed to do. When he comes back he says, we all got to shift our stuff over to that shed. He points. I picks up my bag but then he says, all 'cept them what's here through The Children's Friend Society. Yous lots got to wait here for the lady.

When everybody's gone to that shed there's nine of us left, six young lads, three girls. I don't know none of 'em 'cept one, cove called Rolf who kipped next to me on the ship. We stands there in the sun, not looking at one another. All afraid, trying not to show it. My throat's dry as feathers, I looks round but can't see no water, 'cept in the harbour.

Just when I thinks we're to be left standing til we dries up and blows away, a carriage draws up and a lady steps down. She comes across, looks us up and down. Had you your passages through The Children's Friend Society? she arsks.

Yes Mum, we say.

Where's the other girl?

Mum?

The other girl. I was told to expect four girls.

Please Mum, says one of the girls, there was one took

sick and died. May, that was her name.

Hmm. The lady looks down a paper she's got and says, May Allatt, was *that* the girl?

Yes'm, says the girl who answers before.

Hmm, murmurs the lady again. She don't look happy, but she don't look sad neither. *Vexed* she looks, as if May Allatt died out of spite, to make her job difficult.

The lady calls out our family names, marks her paper as each of us answers. When we done that she folds the list and tells us to follow her. We picks up our bags and trails after her, through streets and streets and streets, til she stops in front of a building which looks like Millbank only not so cheerful.

Cool inside though, which makes us feel better. Me, anyway. We goes into a big room, drops our bags in a corner and sits down at a long table. The lady's gone but another one comes, says, hands together eyes closed, speaks to the lord, but I don't see him cos my eyes is closed. When she's done, women comes in with bowls of soup and tin cups of water, which they sets in front of us. I drains my cup in one go, before starting on the soup, which is the first decent grub I taste since London.

After, a toff comes in and tells us what will happen tomorrow. I'm so tired I can scarcely keep awake let alone understand his talk, which seems to last almost as long as the voyage out. It seems some of us will be put to farm work, some will go into factories, some in domestic service. Something like that. Floor's all the time moving up and down, feels like we're still at sea. Later we traipses through corridors, girls one way, lads another, and comes to a long room with rows of beds both sides. I picks a bed, sets my bag at the foot of it and collapses on the pallet. When I wakes next morning I finds I've slept in my boots.

Nikki

I wake to the creak of the letter-flap, a small thud. Must be morning, though it's still totally dark. I lie listening to the postman's footsteps going away, then remember it's Sunday. No post, and nobody here takes a paper. It's cold and I'm drowsy-warm, so I tell myself it must have been the wind, a gate creaking, the tail end of a dream. I turn over and snuggle down.

I don't know how long afterwards I smell smoke. I know I've slept again, dreamed of sailing round the end of a fixture down the minimarket and bumping into Ronnie. I wake because something's interfering with my breathing, making me cough. Sure for a split second that Ronnie's got me by the throat I sit bolt upright, which shocks me into wakefulness. I can't see anything but it's immediately obvious the room's full of smoke. I swing my feet to the floor, lunge at Demi's bed.

Demi! I choke, *wake up, the house is on fire*. She's awake at once, swinging her legs out, swearing.

Never mind your clothes, she screeches.

I'm crashing about in the dark, trying to find my jeans. My eyes are smarting, streaming. I'm fighting to breathe. The stuff I'm inhaling makes me want to throw up. Demi grabs my hand, tows me towards the door. When she opens it there's sudden, roaring light: the landing's a wall of flame. We reel back, cheeks and noses scorched. I try to scream but vomit instead. You can't scream and throw up at the same time.

The window! croaks Demi. She's got a pair of knickers clamped over her nose and mouth. With her free hand she shoves me across the room. I can hardly see; just enough to make out the pale rectangle where a window-board's missing. Demi winds the knickers round her knuckles and punches out the pane. Go on! she yells. Just *fall*, it's not high.

The middle of the pane has gone, but there are jagged teeth sticking up from the bottom of the frame. I hang back, torn between the dread of disembowelling myself and the desperate need to breathe. Demi's pounding my back, screaming, *go on you silly bitch, you'll kill us both*, but I can't. I *can't*. I'm plucking at the teeth like an inept dentist, trying to extract them with my bare hands. Stay then, she gasps, I'm not. She shoves me aside, falls across the frame and shoves herself out with both hands. Out, and down. There are people under the window, I can hear them.

The instant I'm alone, the need to breathe wins. I flop forward, grasp the sides of the frame, wriggle till there's more of me out than in, and topple. I'm braced for an awful impact but somebody catches me, or at least breaks my fall. Gentle hands lower me on to cold, blessed grass. I hear a siren sinking into darkness, and follow it down.

Nick

Dear Doctor Snow

It seems a long time indeed sins I took my leave of you and embarkt in the New Venture. Much has befallen me and my fellow settlers sins then, some of it too sad to dwell on in this letter, which I trust you'll excuse the liberty of me addresing it to you, but you did make me promise.

We made landfall on October 9th 1855, at Sydney. Of the voyage itself, and indeed of Sydney, the less written the better. Suffice it to say that I was hartily sick when we disembarkt, and hartily glad two days later when I was put in a waggon to begin my journey to Mittagong, which it's eighty miles from the city and not a mile too far in my opinion, tho the journey was uncomftable and took six days. At Mittagong I was put to work on the farm of Mister Bradman, a free settler, and I writes this letter in my little room here, which it's more a sort of shed but ten fousand times better than Sharp's Rents.

It's right, Doctor, what you told me: this Australia is beautiful. (Mister Bradman is a scholard farmer, lends me books. I hopes you notist how better is my spelling and fist, which I works at most every night.) There's space all about: so much space a cove from London can't hold the bigness of Australia in his head. Old Jimmy, the black-fella I works with here, says escape convicts crosses the mountains and walks north looking for China, but never comes to nowhere, not if they walks forever.

There was a lad here before me, Samuel was his name, who saved his wages to buy land. He was just a hungry London boy, now he's got his own farm at a place called Jindalee. I means to follow Samuel's example, dear Doctor. Here in Australia, what you bin don't signify. It's what you can do that counts, and with all this beautiful space to breathe in, a cove comes to feel he can do anything.

I'll close this now, dear Doctor Snow, with a fat white moon over the paddock and work to do tomorrow. May my poor letter come safely to England and find you in good health.

Your servant forever
Nick

Solomon Stern's diary: 12 November 1855

There's a body calling itself The Children's Friend Society, which pays the passages to New South Wales of destitute young persons, including many with criminal records and more no doubt with criminal tendencies. The declared aim of this body is to furnish its youthful beneficiaries with the opportunity to make a fresh start in new surroundings, which it hopes will result in their enjoying better lives in the colony than would be theirs, were they to remain here in England.

I am not acquainted with the lady (I'm told it *is* a lady) who presides over this Society, but if I were I should tell her boldly that she is wasting her time, her fortune and her sympathy. It has been my experience that criminal children become criminal adults, no matter what efforts are expended in misguided attempts to reform them. The only exceptions are those who come to be hanged before attaining maturity.

Criminality is a manifestation of evil, and the evil within a young offender is *not* left wringing its hands at the quayside when its host sails away. What The Children's Friend Society is doing is exporting evil, an activity which is carried out far more economically and with much less misplaced sentimentality by our excellent penal system. We may be sure that the seeds of evil borne in these young breasts to New South Wales will in no case wither in response to the abundance there of sunlight, air and space; rather they will germinate and spread, so that in time the entire colony will become the abode of sin.

The one cause for rejoicing in all of this is that New South Wales lies at a very great distance from England.

Nikki

I mistake that rising dark for death but I've fainted, that's all. I come to in the ambulance; a stranger's face peers into mine. It's all right, she soothes, you inhaled a bit of smoke but you're going to be fine. What with that voice and the siren, I feel like I'm auditioning for *Casualty* and the next line suggests itself. I'm *always* fine after inhaling smoke.

I might have got a laugh out of the cast of *Casualty*. Not this lady. Your friends weren't quite so lucky, she murmurs.

What d'you mean? They're not *dead*?

I try sitting up, she presses me back. No, nobody's dead as far as I'm aware. How many people were in the house?

Six, including me.

Two women, four men?

Yes.

They all got out. The woman gashed herself. Broken glass I think. Neighbours broke her fall, hers and yours. The men jumped round the back, there was nobody to break theirs. Some fractures apparently, I don't know how serious.

Where . . .? I try seeing round her. She restrains me. None of them's riding with you. They're further up the road. Lie back quietly now, we won't be long.

They put me on a trolley, in a corridor. I don't know why they're keeping me – I'm okay, just a bit nauseous. Can't I go? I ask a

220

hurrying nurse. There's nothing wrong with me.

She makes time for a brief smile. Best let *us* decide that, love. Can we contact somebody for you?

It isn't till she asks this that I realize I can't just *go*: my home's on fire and I haven't decided about Mum's yet. I shake my head. No thanks, it's all right. The headshake turns out to be a mistake. Only the nurse's speed keeps my puke from reaching the lino.

After a while a doctor comes, shines a light down my throat and up my nose, tells me they're keeping me overnight for observation. What about the others? I ask. Are they going to be all right?

She nods. They'll be fine Nikki. No broken heads. Just a tibia, an ankle and two collar bones, each on a different patient. Sundry cuts and bruises of course, but nothing's giving us cause for concern. Lucky's what *I've* heard, extremely lucky. She makes to move on.

Doctor?

What is it, Nikki?

I think I know who started the fire.

Did somebody start it?

Yes, I think so.

Oh dear. Well, in cases of that sort the police usually turn up asking questions. Tell them of your suspicions, Nikki. They'll know what to do.

Police. A porter trundles my trolley along the corridor and into a lift. Third floor, he chirps as it lurches to a stop. Ladies' and children's wear, hairdressing, restaurant. He's trying to make me laugh but I'm not in the mood. Maybe that's how the nurse in the ambulance felt.

*

221

They stick me in Women's Medical. Pink frills, shuffling slippers, slack white flesh. Thank goodness it's only one night. Something happens to me in there though, and it's down to other people's visitors.

The first handful walks on to the ward at half-six, and from then till half-eight it's like a procession. There's somebody sitting beside every bed except mine. Some patients have so many visitors there's not enough chairs: guys and kids stand fidgeting, glancing around for something interesting to look at. Adults avoid eye contact with patients, kids stare till told in loud whispers not to.

This sounds pathetic I know, but by about seven o'clock I'm feeling really sorry for myself. I've *chosen* not to tell anybody I'm here; Mum'd come like a shot if she knew. I keep telling myself this but it's no use. Every time somebody walks through the door I look, hoping it's Mum or Gran or somebody I know: a visitor for *me*, even though it's impossible.

I get my visitor at ten to nine, when the others have all gone. It's a policewoman, and I bet she's surprised how ready I am to tell her who I am, and to give my mum's address.

But you were asleep at number nine Fletton Road when it caught fire early this morning, Nikki?

Yes.

Had you a relative there, a friend?

Friends yes, they're all my friends.

Had you been staying with these friends long, Nikki?

Since before Christmas.

And your parents, they knew where you were?

Uh . . . no, no they didn't. Actually it's just my mum, my dad doesn't live with us. Ronnie's not my dad, he's Mum's boyfriend. It's his fault I ran off.

You ran away from home?

Yes.

Before Christmas?

Yes, you've probably been looking for me. Mum'll have reported me missing.

Just a tick. She unclips her radio. Minton, you said, Nikki Minton?

Yes.

The radio crackles, quacks. The policewoman speaks into it, waits, thanks whoever's on the other end, Donald Duck I think, breaks contact, smiles briefly.

My colleague'll contact your mother straight away, Nikki: I expect she'll be here soon. Have you been at Fletton Road ever since you ran away?

No. I slept rough, then stayed with . . . somebody I met.

I see. She stows her radio, resettles herself on the chair. I *really* came to talk to you about the fire, Nikki. There are . . . indications that it might not have been accidental, and we wondered . . .

I interrupt. It *wasn*'t accidental, and I think I know who started it.

Oh?

Yes, I think it was Ronnie.

Would this be the Ronnie you mentioned before? Your mother's boyfriend?

Yes.

And what makes you think he might have started this fire? Why would he do such a thing?

To get rid of me. Arrow says . . .

Arrow?

One of the guys, I don't know his real name. He says Ronnie

might try to put me out of the way so I can't give evidence.

Evidence? What evidence Nikki? You're not making sense.

About the whatsit . . . molesting. He used to touch me, you know, when Mum wasn't there. I told her but she didn't believe me, that's why I ran off. Then he started on my little sister and Mum caught him at it. She chucked him out, reported him. Your colleagues're probably looking for him. Alston, Ronnie Alston.

That gets things moving, I can tell you. By the time Mum arrives, the woman's been on her radio again and there's police running round all over the place. There's going to be an officer on guard outside the ward all night, just like a movie. It's exciting, scary. Mum's all tearful, wants to stay with me but she's left Marie with a neighbour so she can't.

By half-ten everyone's gone, except the night-nurse writing at her desk and the policeman I picture on a chair outside the door, but it isn't quiet. It's amazing the weird noises people in hospital make at night. I try to compose myself for sleep by telling myself it's all over, tomorrow night I'll be in my own little bed, but it doesn't work. In my imagination, Ronnie's climbing a drainpipe right ouside the nearest window, with a knife in his teeth like a pirate. Daft I know, but it makes for a long, long night.

Nikki

I don't get murdered, and Mum's there by half-eight to take me home. She can't though. I've got to wait till after doctor's rounds. It's nearly half-ten when I get the all-clear and they bring my clothes. Mum actually helps me dress, she's so keen. She's had about eight of those vile coffees you get out of a machine and read all the papers, so I don't blame her.

Mum, I say as she holds up my coat, I can't leave without saying ta-ta to Demi and the lads.

Oh Nikki, of *course* you can, she protests as I slip my arms in. They're going to be here for a day or two at least and we're not all that far away. We'll come during visiting hours, this evening if you like.

We?

Yes darling, I'll come too. I'd *like* to meet your friends.

And I let myself be persuaded. I think even then a part of me knew Mum and I wouldn't be back, this or any other evening. Lives have chapters, like books. Events in one chapter may be important because they affect what happens in the next, but we don't go back and re-read it. We move on.

If I want excuses for dropping Demi and the dwarfs, there are plenty to hand. I haven't seen my mother for weeks and weeks, or my little sister. We need to spend time together, there are wounds to bind, but the three of us're hardly out of Mum's beat-up Golf before the police are on the doorstep. Sorry to trouble you, Mrs Minton. We've detained a man answering Ronald Alston's description, but he's refusing to tell us his name or anything else. I wonder if you'd mind coming down to the Station and taking a look?

It *is* Ronnie, which is a relief. I don't see him, I'm at home with Marie. She's going through a bad patch because of what's been happening to her. It's not just what Ronnie did; she's had to be medically examined, specimens taken. DNA and all that. And she's been asked questions about stuff she shouldn't know anything about. The whole thing's left her confused and weepy, which isn't surprising.

The two of us would normally be at school, but Marie's off on doctor's orders and I can't face people once our spot of bother hits the headlines. You know how the tabloids love to rake through people's lives, looking for muck. Weeks before the trial the sharks come sniffing round, and once it starts there's a feeding frenzy. It's unbelievable, there's guys on the garage roof and in the rhododendrons. Anybody entering or leaving our house gets one of those shaggy mikes in the face, and if somebody looks out of a window she's struck blind by flashes. Anybody'd think there were aliens holed up inside, not a pair of little victims.

The trial itself isn't quite the ordeal we've anticipated. I expect it is for Ronnie, but you know what I mean. Marie and I are allowed to give our evidence via a TV link, so we don't have to be in the actual courtroom where he can look at us, and we're whisked to and from the place by a back way, dodging both the press and those sad weirdos who like to lurk outside courts in order to bay at defendants. The trial lasts five days. Ronnie's found not guilty of attempted murder, but guilty of sexual misconduct with minors, arson, and GBH. He gets six years.

I let it happen, weeps Mum, I deserve to go with him.
Like I said, wounds to bind.

Nikki

Little kids are famously resilient, and my sister's no exception. By the time Ronnie's done six weeks of his six years inside she's back at school, socializing and generally picking up where she left off. I wish I could say the same for me.

I try of course, but I soon learn that there are cruel, stupid people out there as well as faithful mates like Kirsty Longthorne.

Kirsty's absolutely terrific from day one. She cares about what Ronnie did to me but she's not *curious*. Our relationship resumes like nothing's happened. She gives me no speculative looks, asks no intrusive questions. Other so-called friends *do*.

First day back at school, I'm really looking forward to catching up with people I haven't seen for ages, especially Janice, Daisy and Philippa. A fortnight has passed since the press lost interest in my family, and Mum's finally persuaded me it's time I got out there and faced the world. These things're always a nine days' wonder, she says. You'll find everybody's more or less forgotten about it by now.

How right she isn't. The three girls come smiling to greet me and there's many a *nice to have you back* which boosts my confidence no end, but as soon as the five of us are safely in our little corner of the yard, Janice is like, well go *on* then Niks, what did he *do*?

I look at her, because at that moment I honestly don't know what she means. What did *who* do? I ask.

You *know*, she goes, winking at Daisy and Philippa, who are smirking in a conspiratorial way. That *pervert*, your mum's boyfriend.

I gaze at her. I can't believe she's asking me this. He molested us, I murmur, feeling my cheeks redden. Marie and me. You knew already, it's been in the papers.

Yeah but like, they never print *details* do they, the papers? I mean, what did he *actually* do? Are you still a . . .

Come *on*, Kirst. I'm hurt and furious at the same time, can't trust myself to speak. I turn, link arms with my friend and we walk away.

Daisy calls after us. Bet you *loved* it Niks, whatever it was. My dad says the girl's *always* asked for it in a case of this sort.

I nearly run home. Kirsty stops me. Ignore them, she says.

But they're my *friends*, Kirst, have been for *years*. How can Daisy's dad *say* something like that about me?

I dunno Niks, I never met the guy but I recognize the type. She snorts. My dad's got a saying about that sort of person: *you can't educate pork*. There's an awful lot of pork out there, Niks.

She tries her very best, old Kirst. It's not her fault it doesn't work out, but it doesn't. Well, if *friends*'re going to treat me like that it's not hard to imagine what neutrals'll do, not to mention enemies. I swear I even catch teachers looking at me funny.

I stick it out for three days. Nobody comes near me if they can help it, and when they have to they don't speak. They're cutting Kirsty as well, of course, for standing by me. When Mum calls up the stairs Thursday morning, I roll over and pull the duvet over my head.

It's not just school. I don't want to leave the house. When I walk along the street I can feel people's eyes watching me through curtained windows. I only have to go into a shop and everybody stops talking. They don't stare, but they fuss over their kids or fiddle with their purses till I've gone. One mother calls sharply to her toddler when I say hello to him by his garden gate. Jack, she snaps, come away, *now*. It doesn't help, I can tell you.

Mum's getting it too. She doesn't talk about it but she's jumpy, irritable. She's trying to be calm and gentle around us, especially Marie, but suddenly she'll lose it and yell, usually at me. *It's all in your mind*, she'll shout, *go to school for God's sake*. Then she'll dash upstairs and cry in her room. When she comes down she'll apologize, say she has a headache. She's getting hassle from the Education Authority about my failure to attend. She can't cope.

In the end she phones her sister. I think I've said Mum and Aunt Steph aren't close. The fact that Mum calls asking a favour shows how desperate she is. It's a big favour too, very big. She's been racking her brains for a way to help me, and come up with a seriously radical idea. What if Nikki gets away, right away to a place where she's not known? Starts over at a new school, makes new friends? What if I can persuade Steph to offer her a home?

She doesn't ask me what *I* think. I've been seeing a shrink, and the bummer about being barmy is, nobody tells you anything. If she'd asked me I'd've told her there was *no* chance of Aunt Steph agreeing to take me in, but I'd've been wrong. I don't know how the conversation went – I was in my room, zonked out on one of the shrink's little pills – but I surface next morning to a done deal. There's just enough dope left in my bloodstream so I don't hit the roof.

And that's how I end up here in West Sussex, living with my snooty Aunt Steph, who isn't all that snooty when you get used to her. The house is near Hayward's Heath but I go to school in Horsham. I've been here three months and nobody's mentioned you know what, which is good because it was doing my head in. Maybe it was the shrink put the idea in Mum's head in the first place, I don't know. If he did, he was right.

It's worked perfectly so far. It's really nice countryside around here. Steph's been alone for years and years so she was ready for a bit of company. I think we can drop the *Aunt*, she says, as we get to know each other over a cup of tea that first afternoon. So she's Steph to me now; we're more like sisters than aunt and niece. I've made new friends at school too, though none of them's quite in Kirsty's league.

It's weird, but all that stuff last winter seems like a dream to me now, inhabited by people I encountered in my sleep. How could they be real, doing the stuff they did, answering to names like Arrow, Monkey and River? Like most people, I prefer not to know too much about how some of my fellow humans live. Unlike most people I've seen it, shared it for a while. My mind shies away from screening those memories in sharp focus. I can just about cope with them blurred.

Kirsty doesn't blur. We talk every day and she texts in between. Here's her text for today: Hi AFEmAI TOY+LUL KIT K

You're the alpha female, Kirst. *I* think of *you* and love *you* lots. And yes, I'll keep in touch.

Letter to the *Sunday Telegraph*

Sir

I am prompted to write by a recent item in my local weekly, to the effect that an entity rejoicing in the name of a Young Person Development Project *has received grant money to finance expeditions to the Lake District by groups of young offenders from deprived estates in the city. The idea apparently is to find out whether experience of a more pleasant environment will have a moderating effect on these youths' behaviour.*

The answer of course is an emphatic no, *and I'll tell you why. Antisocial behaviour is not the by-product of a rundown environment: a rundown environment is the by-product of antisocial behaviour. These deprived estates were once clean, tidy places with wide boulevards, modest but perfectly adequate houses and plenty of green, open spaces. Look at them now.*

My grandfather always used to say, you can take the family out of the slum, but you can't take the slum out of the family. *How right he was!*

It goes without saying that wisdom such as my grandfather's will always be pooh-poohed by politically correct, trendy lefty bodies with names like Young Person Development Project. *I'm afraid that while organizations of this sort hold sway, we will never get to grips with the problem of how to stamp out youth crime in our once great country. Sensitive, touchy-feely policing, offender-friendly juvenile courts and soft, non-custodial sentences having failed, free adventure holidays at taxpayers' expense are to be tried. As Ebenezer Scrooge once said, I'll retire to Bedlam.*

Yours sincerely
Cleasby Nossiter

Letter to Nick Webley

My Dear Young Friend

Words cannot express adequately my delight on reading your last letter, which reached my hand on the sixteenth of March. How totally your life has been transformed in the few years since you left London! Your remarks regarding my *part in all of this are over-generous by the way. Everything you have achieved, you have achieved by your own courage, resourcefulness and unmitigated hard work.*

Cootamundry is a town I'd not heard of till I had your letter; Mittangong is better known here. Still, I suppose a move of one hundred and fifty miles seems nothing in so vast a land. Certainly the move you made simultaneously from labourer to landowner was far greater. Forty acres, *Nick! What a triumph, and how richly deserved. The labour necessary to clear so extensive a holding must be little short of Herculean, and with your closest neighbour four miles away, I fancy loneliness is an added burden. I hope that it will not be too long before you are in a position to have a labourer on your land, and a helpmeet in your house.*

My own progress, though less spectacular, is nevertheless satisfying in its way. The evidence I was able to assemble, following the outbreak which carried off your precious family, has at long last convinced the powers-that-be of the connection between cholera and contaminated water. Miasma theory is dead, and work has been put in hand to drain the worst of our cesspools. In due course a system of new pipes will carry clean water to every part of the city, and it is reported that similar projects are in hand in other parts of the country. In short, my idea stands vindicated, and I feel confident that the scourge of cholera will soon be lifted from the land. The Almighty will no doubt devise other ways to punish sin.

I called on Jack Kaggs as you asked me to, Nick, and had the inestimable pleasure of surprising and delighting him with the news of your triumph. He told me he knew you'd be a toff some day because of your fondness for big words. He is hale and hearty, and his wife continues well also.

In closing this letter, let me tell you what I will see in my mind's eye whenever I think of you. I'll see mountains, blue with distance, beyond a vista of tree-clad, rolling hills. Closer, stretching away to where the hills begin is a vast plain, drenched in golden light and dotted with unfamiliar trees. In the foreground a man leans on a fence of sun-bleached rails, gazing out over his land. He was born neither good nor bad. His thoughts are deep thoughts because he is an auto-didact, a self-taught scholar. The fence is a sturdy one, and his house is well made too for he wrought them both himself, and he is the son of a carpenter.

Your friend
John